SHATTERED

THE TORZIAL AFFAIR BOOK 1

VIA MARI

CONTENTS

TRIGGER WARNING!

In Degrees of Acceptance, A Prestian Series book, Katarina's best friend Jenny Torzial was raped by a man she trusted. I contemplated sharing Jenny's story throughout the next books of that series, but decided instead to dedicate an entirely new one to her journey.

The effects of such trauma are different for many individuals and the way each deal with these impacts is as unique as they are. Jenny is a strong, independent woman who was traumatized while in a vanilla relationship with a man she believed would someday be her husband.

In this series, she journeys through her pain and fears. Jenny is taken on a non-vanilla sexual exploration which allows her to discover a life she has only dreamt about in the past, allowing her to trust and to love again.

The Torzial Series deals with rape, which may be offensive

or a trigger to certain readers. I felt compelled to tell Jenny's story for the readers who fell in love with her in The Prestian Series and hope you will find that it was written with a great deal of thought and compassion. It does contain scenes of non-consensual bondage, consensual bondage, and spanking, so please consider this prior to reading.

<u>SHATTERED</u>

ONE
JENNY

C hase and Kate say their vows in front of only their closest friends and family and I see her dad, head of the East Coast crime syndicate, discreetly wipe away a tear from her mom's face as the bride and groom exchange rings. When the officiant pronounces them husband and wife, Chase draws Kate into his arms and kisses her with a passion that leaves me slightly embarrassed before the room bursts into celebration and cameras begin to flash.

The tall man standing next to me grins showing a perfect set of bright white teeth and claps Chase on the back as he and Kate join us a few moments later. "Congratulations," he says.

"Thanks, Brian, I'm glad you were able to make it," Chase says, smiling widely.

"Sorry it was so late and I couldn't be at the dinner last

night. Negotiations were a little more difficult than anticipated," Brian says.

"Congratulations, you look so happy and absolutely beautiful," I say to Kate as Chase relinquishes his bride for a moment so that I can hug her tight.

"I know its cliché, but I really couldn't be happier and you look gorgeous yourself. The sapphire color of that gown looks amazing with your long dark hair," she whispers before Chase returns his arm to his new bride's waist.

"We were just about to sub you with one of Katarina's uncles. The big burly bald one," Chase says to Brian, motioning to the other side of the stairs.

Brian smirks at Chase and turns to Kate. "You look absolutely lovely," he says, kissing her cheek.

"Thank you. Pretty sure Chase is just teasing. We probably would have picked Uncle Vito to stand in. Same height, look, well, you know, and then you would owe him your right arm," she says, amusement lighting up in her eyes. Uncle Vito must be extremely tall to be any match at all for this intimidating man who wears the themed black suit and sapphire tie comfortably. He must be at least six foot two or three with a full head of dark jet black hair, but it's his eyes that make it hard for me to turn away.

Brian laughs at Kate's joke, but as if he can sense my gaze, turns the full concentration of those shocking blue eyes on me as Chase officially introduces us. "Brian, this is Jenny Torzial,

Katarina's best friend, and the maid of honor, and Brian is my best man and currently the chief operating officer for Prestian Corp," Chase says.

Brian levels me with his gaze. "That Jenny. Well it's nice to meet you in person, Ms. Torzial," he says, extending a well-manicured hand. His fingers close around mine and his touch creates a tingling sensation that causes my skin to heat.

"Likewise, Brian," I say as he lets go of my hand. The band begins to play the first song and Chase excuses himself to lead Kate across the great room of the Larussio mansion, which has been turned into a vast marble ballroom for the event.

"I'm glad everything is working out so well for them. I never thought Kate would let anyone get close enough to even develop a relationship, much less get married," I say.

"I have to admit Chase settling down was quite a surprise, too," Brian says.

"It's heartwarming that her dad could give her away. She never even knew him until a few months ago," I say, trying to pull my eyes away from the blue intensity of his.

"That's what I understand. I'm glad to see Chase met someone that makes him happy," Brian says, breaking our gaze as we turn to watch Kate's dad step in for a dance with his daughter. They sway to the music for the majority of the song but as he spins her for the last chorus I see him gently wipe a tear from her eye.

"Our turn," Brian says, leading me onto the floor as the MC

announces the best man and maid of honor dance. The song is embarrassingly slow, created for lovers, and I feel my breath hitch and skin quiver as he draws me close, the fresh scent of his soap and musky cologne filling my senses as he skillfully guides me across the floor. The pull of his crystalline gaze makes me look up and my cheeks warm at the intensity reflected in his twinkling blue eyes, as I try desperately to ignore the electricity his thumb is creating as it circles the inside of my palm.

"You're stunning. I'm the envy of every man in this room right now," Brian says, slipping his hand underneath my hair and around the nape of my neck causing my pulse to race. The warmth of his breath against my hair, and the fingers gently caressing the back of my neck before settling at my waist cause goosebumps on my arms and sends a tingling sensation down my spine. It's clearly been too long since I was this close to someone of the opposite sex.

"Thank you," I say somewhat breathlessly, finding it difficult to respond as his hand gently tightens around my own. I try to concentrate on the dance steps as he holds me close and all sense of time is gone as he guides me effortlessly to the popular ballad and begins twirling me for the final chorus. As the song finishes, he places his arm around my waist and guides me from the dance floor to the full-length bar on the other side of the great room.

He holds out my chair and orders drinks for both of us. I hold my tongue at his presumptuousness and as the flavor touches my lips and swirls around my tongue a murmur of approval escapes me. "This is wonderful," I admit, letting the taste resonate before swallowing. It is a crisp white wine with a wonderfully sweet although complex balance.

"It has a layered quality, full bodied and elegant. Carlos has a palette for great wine," he says as his eyes wander from my glass lower.

"Do you know him well?" I ask, feeling the heat his eyes on my chest is creating.

"Our families have mutual business interests but I don't know him well," he says.

"I've met Jenny's mom several times over the years, but like Kate, just met Carlos earlier in the year," I say.

"Chase tells me you'll be working on all of his facilities and some for Carlos, too," Brian says, swirling his drink as he regards me.

"Yes, we're currently under contract for the expansions of the Prestian Medical Facilities and Carlos is looking for assistance with some developments in Vegas as well," I say.

"Your company's work in lean and efficiency is good. I've been extremely impressed with the forecasting analytics," he says.

"Thank you," I say, taking another sip of my wine, trying desperately to focus on something, anything other than my rapid pulse.

He uses one finger to raise my chin, leaving me no choice

but to look into his crystalline blue eyes. They are the most intense color, smoldering and smoky, now holding my own completely captivated. "Dance with me," he says, setting my wine glass on the bar before guiding me onto the floor as the band extends an invitation to everyone.

Brian pulls me close and with his hand, places my head on his chest. I can feel the strong beat of his heart against my cheek and the warmth of his breath in my hair. He skillfully weaves me around the dance floor now dotted with family and friends. "I like the way you feel in my arms," he says quietly, while his finger continues tracing a circular pattern on the small of my back.

"Me, too," I say, my cheeks flaming as I feel my nipples harden against him through the thin material of my dress.

He keeps me pressed close. "I can feel how turned on you are. What's the flushed little face about? Are you embarrassed?" he whispers in my ear.

I feel myself moistening and only contemplate a moment before responding. "Yes," I say, my voice barely above a whisper.

"Why does it embarrass you?" he asks, his eyes holding mine as he looks down at me.

"Maybe I thought I was the only one who felt it," I say breathlessly.

"You can't feel my cock pressed against your thigh as I guide you around the dance floor?" he asks quietly.

I look down and away from him, feeling the warmth of my cheeks deepen further. "Yes," I say, now completely focused on the feel of it against me.

"Your downcast eyes are exciting, all submissive-like, but right now I want to see those deep green eyes looking at me so I can tell what you're feeling," he says, lifting and tilting my chin.

"Are you always this forward?" I ask.

"Yes. I have no desire to play games. So we've cleared up that you're not the only one aroused?" he asks, his mouth quirking to the side as he awaits my answer.

"Pretty sure you've covered that," I say, mesmerized by the seas of blue that feel like they penetrate right through me.

"Good," he says, guiding me off the dance floor to our seats at the bar.

"So are there any best man and maid of honor protocols we need to adhere to this evening?" I ask as I reach for my drink.

"In terms of responsibilities to the bride and groom or to each other?" he asks.

"My question was more related to the wedding as a whole," I say, taking a sip of my wine and trying not to look up as I feel the intensity of his gaze upon me.

"No protocol that I know of but I'm pretty certain a kiss is almost always common place between the best man and maid of honor," he says.

I look up at that and see the amusement in his eyes. "You're having fun at my expense."

"No, I'm letting you know what to expect. A shout out over the bow if you will," he says.

"Are you always so presuming?" I ask.

He levels me with a look. "As before, I have no interest in games. You're gorgeous, you feel the attraction, too, and before the end of this evening, I do plan to kiss you," he says.

My breath catches. It's been months since I've been with anyone physically and it's impossible to deny the attraction. I find it difficult to look away from the heat of his gaze. "Since we're not playing games, I'd like that very much," I say softly, immediately appalled that I've managed to express this aloud without a shred of embarrassment.

"Come with me," he says, guiding me with a hand on the small of my back past the throng of dancers spread out across the marble floor, down the hall, and into an empty study. The door has barely closed before he pulls me into his arms. My breath shallows and body tingles as his hand cradles the back of my neck, holding me still for a moment, his eyes wordlessly asking before his mouth descends and connects with my own. His tongue circles my lips, teasing me until I open for him. He is not gentle but instead demanding. My tongue entwines with his of its own accord welcoming the sensual feel of the intimate connection, enthralled with a passion I've always longed for but never felt. His hand cups my breast, his thumb instinctively finding and caressing the aroused nipple poking through the thin material. He takes the captured nub between his thumb and fore-finger, squeezing until I moan with the feel it creates in my center. I hear myself softly moan again, pushing against the arousal that's firmly pressed against my lower belly.

"Still think you're the only one that feels the attraction?" he asks, repositioning himself so I feel the entire length of his cock along my hip bone.

I shake my head, my own body moistening at the feel of his desire pushed against me. He takes my hands, sliding them up the wall, holding them securely above my head as his tongue continues its exploration. As the constriction of my wrists resonates in my brain, my pulse accelerates and I am suddenly overcome with mind-gripping fear. My heart begins to beat wildly and survival instinct takes over. I yank my wrists as hard as possible at the same time my knee connects with his groin, allowing me to free myself from the strength of his hold.

I use that moment to bolt, yanking open the door and all I hear is, "Christ! What the hell," as I tear out of the study, making my way down the empty hall to the back stairs, taking them two at a time, all the way to the top, slamming the door behind me before sinking into a sobbing pile on the floor. I don't know how long it takes before my breathing and heart rate slow down, although finally they do, enough for me to make my way to the queen-sized bed and bury my head into the comforting depths of the feather pillow. I wipe the tears which continue to fall for the next hour or so before I've completely calmed down and nothing is left but mortification and embarrassment for my behavior.

Brian must think I'm seriously unstable and maybe I am. I

don't know how to put it into words but I know he deserves an explanation. I finally grab my phone and begin typing an email, deleting the first few drafts before settling on the final version and hitting the send button.

TWO

BRIAN

She tears out of the room. What the fuck! Lucky for me there's a height difference and her aim wasn't perfect. I take a few moments to adjust myself and let the hard-on in my pants settle before heading to the great room. Jenny is nowhere to be seen. I mingle for a while doing my best to socialize, when in reality all I want is to find her and spank that luscious little ass until she can't sit down for a week. I make a few more rounds and talk with Chase's father, Don Prestian, and Kate's father, Carlos Larussio, before saying good night to Chase and Kate and texting my driver to have the car brought around.

He pulls up just as I exit the Larussio estate, the valet opens the door of the sleek black limousine, and I slide into the back seat. "We'll be staying in the city tonight, Wes," I say.

"Excellent. It feels good to be stateside after being out of the country for the last couple weeks," he says.

"It sure does," I say before pushing the button on the door to engage the privacy glass.

We have barely started moving before I'm on my cell to Scottie, head of security for Carrington Steel Industries. "I need an in-depth profile on Jennifer Torzial, owner of Torzial Consulting Firm and I need it as quick as you can get it pulled together," I say.

"I'll try to have it in your hands by morning. Need anything else?" he asks.

"No, that's all for now. Have a good evening," I say before disconnecting. I am deep in thought when a text message distracts me.

Message: Heard you were back in New York and thought you may be lonely on Christmas Eve.

I sigh. Sasha Koslov, a lovely long-legged blonde with high-sitting perky little tits who knew exactly how to keep a man like me entertained. The way she begged and moaned kept me interested for hours the first time, and unlike the others, I let her have a second and a third. A mistake, she was just like everyone else, wanting a personal bond, some sort of emotional connection. I don't do relationships. They all know what they're getting into up front, but as soon as they realize I'm the heir of the Carrington Steel Empire, all of a sudden, every fucking one of them wants more. It's been a month since I broke it off. I was hoping she would have moved on by now.

Reply: I'm back in NY, but not alone or lonely.

I hit the send button and grimace at the coldness of the message, a flicker of shame briefly washing over me at the blatant lie, but she obviously needs confirmation it's over.

I'm restless after the encounter with Jenny and briefly consider calling her. She was clearly aroused, so damn responsive and even an attempted kick to the balls couldn't get my raging hard-on to go down right away. My cock twitches at the mere thought of her hard little nipples pressed against me and the way her breath hitched when I lifted her chin and forced her to look in my eyes. And that damned blush. I'd love nothing better than to turn her over my knee and watch her ass go from light to dark pink and then red as she begs me to forgive her before fucking her senseless for what she did tonight.

The sliding privacy panel between the front seats and passenger comes down, pulling me out of my reverie.

"Brian, we've got paparazzi camped out everywhere. Security has them contained, but I'm afraid they're not leaving," Wes says.

"It's fine, the story was sure to break at some point. What better timing than Christmas Eve," I say dryly, knowing that Sasha has been talking with the paparazzi and wondering if she's still negotiating a price for a story. She was under a nondisclosure agreement but only related to sexual content. What she says to the paparazzi outside of that is her business.

"I'll drop you off at the front entrance. The security team

will have you surrounded the minute you step out of the car," he says.

"Thanks, Wes," I say, straightening my tie before the limo stops and the door is opened. The security team instantly flanks me as I head toward the entrance of the Carrington sky-rise and the paparazzi begin shooting rapid fire questions. "Is it true you attended the private wedding of long-time entrepreneur Chase Prestian this evening? Is it true you are no longer dating Sasha Koslov the Russian Ballerina?" I grimace, loathing the brassiness of the reporter and ignore the questions, looking around instead at the crowd.

I nod to the lady with her hand raised. "We appreciate you taking the time to spend a few moments with us on Christmas Eve. Anything you can share about Chase Prestian's wedding or your relationship with Sasha that you don't mind having publicly disclosed?"

Smooth and polished. I like her approach. I nod, gesturing for her and the camera crew to come forward and hold out my hand for the mic. "I can confirm that Chase Prestian and Katarina Meilers-Larussio were married this evening, it was a small private wedding shared with family and friends at the Larussio estate, and I was honored to stand up for Chase as his best man. As for Sasha Koslov, she and I went to a couple of charity functions together," I say.

"Can you confirm if Larussio family members from Italy were present at the wedding?" one of the other news reporters asks.

"That's a wrap folks. I hope you have enough to go home and spend time with your families. Have a good evening," I say, handing the mic back to the red-haired journalist before heading inside and towards the private elevator. "Find out the name of the ginger," I say to Paulie and Vitrie who step into the elevator behind me and key in the code for the penthouse.

"Will do Brian, your quarters have been cleared," Devon, another security guard says.

"Thanks, I'll be glad when everything settles down. The level of security Chase is demanding for all of Prestian Corp executives, family, and friends is becoming a serious pain in the ass," I say.

"No worries from our end. We've been briefed about Alfreita and he won't get close to anyone on our watch," Devon says. He is formidable and dwarfs me even at my six-foot-two inches.

Paulie is smiling widely. "Scottie said Jay's been calling him constantly with updates and questions, but no news yet," he says.

"And that makes you smile?" I ask.

"Seriously, someone questioning Scottie? He's probably in a flipping tiz," he says, trying to keep his amusement in check.

I nod, smirking at the thought myself. "Well, let's hope it's over soon and thanks for your help this evening," I say, hoping that Jay, Chase's head of security, has things wrapped up with Alfreita soon. The elevator displays the ninetieth floor and opens into my penthouse.

The fireplace is going and the city lights of New York shine through the floor-to-ceiling corner expanses of glass that serve as two walls of the home. I head to the chrome and glass bar and pour myself a glass of scotch and look out over Manhattan to one side and Central Park to the other. What the hell happened tonight? One minute I had a warm blooded responsive woman in my arms, kissing me with such passion I could hardly breathe and the next she's trying desperately to kick me in the nuts and disappears. What the fuck! I decide to text Chase and give him a heads up on the news story.

Message: Paparazzi was camped out tonight. Gave them the story we discussed.

Reply: SG.

I laugh at my best friend who is usually always so formal, the man who took me under his wing after I finished college and has mentored me in the position of COO for Prestian Corp for the last five years in preparation for taking over as CEO of the empire left to me when my parents died. SG. Sounds good. I wonder if Kate taught him that.

I shrug out of my suit jacket and throw it over the dining room chair before settling in at the desk trying to shake my mood. I nurse my drink while looking out over New York as the Mac loads and skim emails once it does. The message from Jenny catches my attention, sent just an hour ago.

Brian,

I owe you an apology. Please know that you did absolutely nothing wrong. I am sorry for my behavior. I sincerely hope it will not affect our working relationship and that you can forgive me.

Jenny

I read it again. The note contains nothing which would give me a goddamn clue as to what's going on with her. I shake my head and decide not to respond tonight. Her note makes me smile. She thinks I can do damage to her reputation as the COO of Prestian Corp. She clearly has no idea who I really am. I take another pull of my drink, smiling at the irony. Most women will stop at nothing, clamoring to get my attention even when they think I'm just the COO of Prestian Corp. She has my interest and tries to kick me in the nuts.

I wake to the ping of my cell and glance at my phone's screen, reading the message from Scottie.

Message: Profile summary is in your inbox. Merry Christmas!

I grab my notebook from the nightstand and open the PDF he's sent, skimming through the first few pages noting that her middle name is Ann, she's twenty-eight and born on April 10th. Family consists of a mother, two aunts, a brother, a sister, two nieces and one nephew. Father died before she graduated high school from a heart attack. I skim to the end and flip to the next page surprised by her education. Started her own business fresh out of high school offering project planning and consultant advice to small companies all while attending N.Y. University online.

Scottie has included pictures of her graduation ceremonies accepting top of her class for both her Bachelor's and Master's. I zoom in on the pictures and find myself staring into those deep green eyes looking back at me. My cock twitches. I move to the next page.

Her bank statements are remarkable. Very conservative, doesn't buy much for herself and deposited all the profits back into the bank along with her part of her father's inheritance. After graduation she invested in an upscale business rental and added design consulting to her company's offerings. I flip back and forth between her activity and bank statements. Damn, very impressive. She managed to triple her father's inheritance and get two degrees by the time she was twenty four. I skim through parts of the detailed document. She hired Katarina Meilers as an entry level employee after she graduated from high school. I do the math; they've been working together for about seven years.

I scan over all of Katarina's work advancements until I get to Scottie's notes about Chase. I sit up and slide against the bed's headboard. Shit, I knew Chase invested in Torzial, and that an entire division of the company is dedicated to the Prestian Corp Medical facilities. I even knew he created shared services for certain parts of the division, but what I didn't know was the size of the start-up he invested in, all off the books or I would have seen it before. I read through the contract agreements Scottie has included and let out a low whistle as I skim over Chase's outlay and future projections for return. I can see why it would be a win for both companies.

I skip to the next page. No real relationships in her life until she began dating Ty Channing, a corporate lawyer, and they were exclusive until one night a few months ago. Medical history shows she has a physical every year, goes to the dentist twice a year, an ophthalmologist once a year, enjoys yoga three nights a week at a local club, and began therapy with an upscale counselor in Chicago two weeks after her relationship ended. My fists clench at my side reading this. I need to know exactly what and why she reacted the way she did last night.

Message: Can you start a detailed summary on Ty?

Reply: Already on it. Figured you'd want it.

Message: Thanks. I want to know everything..

THREE

JENNY

I'm awakened by sounds around me and my cheeks warm with embarrassment as the bed in the suite next to mine begins creaking steady and strong. It's not hard to imagine what's going on behind the walls of the next room. Newlyweds!

I go into the suite's kitchenette to get a drink and then into the bathroom. I'm washing my hands when I hear a loud rhythmic thumping and the bathroom picture of lilacs shifts and becomes crooked. I can't contain my laughter as I realize what's going on in both of the rooms on either side of me. I'm clearly the only one not having sex tonight! I crawl back into bed and my mind drifts back to earlier, wondering what would have happened between Brian and me if I hadn't freaked out. The crystalline sea colored eyes and his mouth crushing mine is all I can think about, that and the moisture between my legs as I recall it. The headboard pounds against the wall of my bedroom and I hear Kate moan. I bite my lip grinning, wondering if she'll even be able to walk tomorrow. I finally put my headphones in to drown it all out before eventually falling back to sleep.

* * *

I wake groggy and unrested, skimming my phone for a message from Brian. It was Christmas Eve, so maybe unlike me he actually signs off email for the holidays. I get washed up, dressed, and head downstairs to the kitchen. Kate is curled up in Chase's lap and he is kissing her neck.

"Are you two at it again?" I say, grinning at Kate as I walk towards the dining room table laughing as I listen to the two couples bantering about the night before.

Chase grins widely, clearly amused. "So it would appear we're off to a wonderful Christmas Eve tradition," he says, taking Kate's hand as she reddens and shakes her head at his reference to the sex going on around me last evening.

"Indeed it does," her father says, beaming down at Karissa.

Chase takes pity on his new mother-in-law and changes topics of conversation to plans for the day as we finish our meal.

"Service will be starting shortly," Carlos says, leading us into the great room. The transformation is phenomenal. Where a bar was the previous night, a pulpit stands, the same lights and Christmas tree remain, but nativity statues have been brought in along with poinsettias, which have been placed on each of the marbled stairs of the curved staircase. Chairs have been set up just like church and the family that partook in our festivities last night files in along with Don and Emily, her daughter and son-in-law, and grandchildren. The officiant that married Kate and Chase last night presides over Carlos's family's Christmas sermon this morning. The wealth of this family never ceases to amaze me. Unbelievable what money can buy.

M att comes into the kitchen after a boisterous and fun family lunch that is served with plenty of wine and toasts. "The helicopter just landed. It'll take us to the jet whenever you're ready," he says.

"Okay, we'll take off shortly after Chase and Kate," I say before turning to Kate. "I hope you have a wonderful honeymoon and I'll see you when you get back," I say, hugging my best friend tight as she prepares to leave.

"She'll have a great time, I'll make sure of it," Chase says, smirking.

"You better!" I say, narrowing my eyes at him in jest before Matt escorts me to the helipad and assists me into the luxurious custom cabin of the Prestian Corp helicopter.

The flight to the airport is uneventful, but as we get out of the helicopter at the airport we are immediately surrounded by security. "What's going on?" I ask Matt.

"I'm not really at liberty to disclose too much but everything's under control," he says.

"You have to tell me what's going on. Our security has doubled."

"You need to text Chase if you want details."

"That's seriously annoying as hell," I huff.

"My job is to keep you safe and you're not making it any easier," he says flatly.

I grimace at the look on his face, immediately remorseful knowing full well the extent the entire team has gone to in order to keep us all protected. "Sorry, Matt. I'm really not trying to be a pain in the ass," I say as we're escorted by security up the ramp and into the awaiting Gulfstream. We chat a moment with the captain and crew before the guards disperse into the private area behind the flight crew and Matt closes the door behind us as we continue into the main cabin.

It's just one of the many jets in the Prestian Corp fleet and this one is decorated in light beige colored furniture. A long leather couch is in front of a stone fireplace, with matching recliners on either side of it. I sink into the soft leather recliner adjacent to the fire and open my MacBook before signing onto the plane's Wi-Fi to skim emails. No response from Brian. It shouldn't bother me but it does.

It's not long before we take off, circling around the Manhattan city scape leaving Lady Liberty behind. I unbuckle and head into the back bedroom hoping for an amazing mile high nap after my restless night. I set my alarm for the two hour flight to Chicago, slip out of my flats and crawl under the covers before falling into a deep sleep, leaving all the chaos of the last couple days behind me. The alarm goes off and I've easily managed to sleep through the entire trip. I scurry into the bathroom to freshen up before finding Matt reading a magazine and intermittently texting on his phone in the main cabin.

"You get cell service up here?" I ask as I watch him pound out text after text, scowling.

"Yeah, special package. You can sign on to the main server overhead with the public password if you need to check email or anything," he says.

"Nothing I do business wise is so important it can't wait two hours. I was just curious about how you could text," I say, pulling out my laptop and for the third time this afternoon checking email.

"It sure doesn't look like you can wait two hours. You need me to text someone for you?" Matt asks, smirking.

I scowl at him. "Smart ass!"

I'm not sure why I thought Brian would send me a note after the way I behaved, but deep down, I was hoping that he would. I peruse through the others and groan, replying to the numerous notes asking for bids on new work from people that have ties to the Prestian Corporation. At this rate, Torzial will definitely need to keep expanding. It's a good thing and I know it, but everything is happening ten times faster now that Chase Prestian is involved.

"We'll be landing in ten minutes," the pilot says over the

speaker system, just as I finish sending out the last of the pricing quotes. The Gulfstream touches down and makes its way to the private tarmac. Matt and I are immediately surrounded by a security team as he guides me down the ramp to the awaiting car, and then joins me in the back seat for the ride home.

"You're staying at my house tonight?" I ask, used to having Chase's security with me.

"Sorry, you're stuck with me, boss's orders," he says wryly.

"You know I wasn't being sarcastic. I really appreciate you hanging out with me. Do you know when everything will settle down with Alfreita?" I ask.

"I wish I did, but until it does we need to make sure anyone closely connected with Chase and Kate have a very high level of security. It would actually make me feel a lot better if you would agree to stay at Chase's. He's got a hell of a lot better security system than yours," he says.

"I know Matt, but I don't want to impose and besides, you know the place we looked at before we left for my mom's? They accepted my offer! You're now looking at the proud owner of a condo close enough that I can actually walk to Torzial," I say.

"Sweet. That forty-minute drive back and forth is a pain in the ass now that you're located at Prestian Corp. Did you let Chase know so he could have his security team check it out?" he says.

I narrow my eyes at him. "No, I did not. It is much safer than my house. It has a secure entrance, a doorman, and some sort of security system throughout. Plus, I owe him enough and this I am doing on my own," I say.

"Alright, I'll let you explain it to him then. I thought we'd be flying back out by your family after the wedding. You know, it is Christmas," he says.

"The time we spent with them before the wedding was plenty. I'm just sorry you have to babysit me on Christmas day," I say.

"It's not a thing, Jenny. I don't have any family other than Chase and the guys. I'll hit the couch tonight, if that's okay," he says.

"Thanks, Matt," I say as our driver navigates the limo out of O'Hare and into the early evening traffic. It is not nearly as congested as normal due to the holiday. I settle back for the ride across town and glance at my phone. Almost five p.m., dusk is settling in and the lights are beginning to twinkle across the city.

"Can you stop for wine?" I say to the driver.

"Matt, the itinerary doesn't include a stop. Any issues with protocol?" he says, glancing in the rearview mirror.

"Fuck yeah, but let's do it anyway. I'll let security know and go in with her myself," he says, scowling at me.

I narrow my eyes at him. "Thanks. I don't have any left at home and didn't think you'd want me to go back out tonight," I say.

"You roaming the streets of Chicago isn't going to happen," he says, as the driver opens our door.

FOUR

BRIAN

I wake at four a.m. and like every Christmas morning since my father died I feel the ache of loneliness. It's only been ten years since he's passed, but it seems like a lifetime ago. I stretch and pull on running clothes before heading to the penthouse gym.

Even the expansive view of Central Park which normally calms me doesn't rid me of my restlessness. I can't help thinking about the night before and Jenny, how her skin and body felt pressed against me. So soft to the touch, white and creamy, and her eyes, deep green pools that a man could drown in, her hair, long dark smooth tresses that gently curl in folds down her shoulders and lie in layers over the swell of her perky little breasts. I crank up the treadmill and push myself even harder as I think about last night. My desire for her, the way her lips opened to me, letting me explore her depths. The gentle sound she made when I cupped her breast and her moan when I pinched her nipples between my fingers. Jesus, she physically pushed into my hardness when she felt that. I know she wanted me, damn it! I get off the treadmill an hour later dripping in sweat and send a message to Scottie.

Message: Ty's report?

Reply: Almost done.

I feel like a jackass knowing it's Christmas even though Scottie doesn't have a family. I shed my clothes and head into the wrap-around stone shower letting the water pummel me. The dual showerheads help to alleviate some of the stress in my muscles before I step out, get dressed for the day, and head into the kitchen for breakfast.

I open the large stainless steel refrigerator and pull out what I'm looking for. Celia has left an egg bake casserole for breakfast with instructions for heating. Every Christmas Eve day she insists on baking it in preparation for Christmas morning before I fly her out to spend time with her children and grandkids. I scoop a large dish onto a plate, place it into the microwave to heat and throw a K-Cup into the Keurig while I wait. I smile, recalling the first time she taught me how to use the damn thing. Who knew you needed to add the water yourself. High maintenance little gadget but damned if it doesn't make the perfect cup of coffee.

I settle in at the kitchen table with breakfast, opening my Mac and skimming investment stocks until I hear the familiar ding of an incoming message. Finally! My cell rings at almost the same exact time and I answer it immediately. "Just got your summary. Were you going to give me a chance to read it?" I say.

"Yeah, well, I wanted to give you an update verbally, too."

"That bad?" I ask.

"Lad, whatever's going on it's nothing you want to get into the middle of. The guy's a corporate lawyer and until recently represented four of the top five pharmaceutical companies. I sent you their names and you can look at the details later, but basically his bank accounts show receipt of wired transfers of five million dollars apiece by each of the companies a few months ago, but then all the funds were transferred back to the pharmaceutical companies a few days later.

"Embezzling? Laundering?"

"So far laundering for sure and we're looking into whose. We're not sure why he sent the pharm money back," Scottie says.

"What the fuck does that have to do with Jenny?" I ask.

"The day before the money was transferred back, Chase Prestian and Kate Meilers- Larussio went to meet with Jenny and Ty at the Torzial firm in Chicago. Chase and Kate left a short while later and they were heavily flanked by Prestian Corp security. Jenny and Ty left the building shortly after that. Jenny's credit card shows a cab charge a few hours later leaving his condo back to her own house. It was only odd since she hadn't stayed at her own place in months."

My heart is racing at the thought of what may have gone

down and for some unexplainable reason I press him. "Tell me what happened," I say between gritted teeth.

"A few of my guys know some people and they looked into taxi records. It's fucking Chicago, right? They keep an internal register in case the police, or worse, come snooping around. The cabbie logged her in with a split lip. She gave him her address, but didn't talk the entire drive to her place. He figured she and her significant other had been in a fight, didn't get into a conversation about it but did document it just in case it came back to bite him. About an hour later, Kate's being escorted to Jenny's place."

Fuck me! I try to shake the thought of her delicate cotton candy colored little lips being split open. My entire body is filled with rage at the thought of that asshole's hands anywhere near her. I can't explain why, but I need to hear the rest and prompt him to continue.

"A few hours later, Jay, Chase's head of security sends in a couple guys to watch the neighborhood, and Matt, her current security detail stays with her overnight while another of Jay's guys takes Kate back to Prestian's condo. After that, all hell breaks loose, Brian. Police records show that a burglary alarm went off at Ty's office. The camera in his sky-rise shows him leaving, getting into a private car and going to his office uptown. Those same cameras went off the grid for about ten minutes a short time later and then again an hour later."

"What the fuck!"

"Yeah, now the light's coming on. This is not something

you want to be involved in Brian. The next day all the money Ty received was returned to the pharmaceutical companies. It looks legit on paper but as soon as I saw the money flow I traced it dirty. He fucked around with Carlos Larussio's daughter's best friend. A couple days later, someone broke into his condo, beat him to within an inch of his life and left him with a mafia cut across the neck that should have killed him. He was in the hospital for weeks. Whatever happened that afternoon and evening caused Jennifer to leave Ty and the mafia to come after him. You saw the other report; she went into counseling two weeks later. I'm trying to get the details now," he says.

"I'll read the detailed report. Thanks for getting it done so fast. Is she still at the Larussio's?"

"Yes, she stayed the night."

"Thanks, Scottie. Have a Merry Christmas," I say before disconnecting.

I am bored and restless, the same thing every year. I look around at the spacious room and briefly contemplate calling her, seeing if she'd like to go to Rockefeller Center, but then just as quickly abandon the idea. She is spending time with the Larussios and Chase and Kate have probably already headed out for their honeymoon. There's nothing here for me today. I might as well spend it in the air and get some work done.

Message: I need to be in Chicago as quickly as possible.

Reply: The plane is on the concourse and I'll have the helicopter pick you up on the helipad in twenty minutes.

Message: Excellent. Let me know when she's on the move again.

Reply: I'll put someone on it right away.

Message: You gave Wes the day off, you want me to have him meet you or are you okay with security driving?

Reply: Security is fine.

Message: "Merry Christmas, Brian."

I finish my coffee, grab my coat and laptop bag, turn off the lights and get into the elevator for the ride to the helipad on the top of my building. The helicopter veers out over the bay, around the perimeter of the city, and towards the airport. It takes less than ten minutes in the air before I am being escorted to the awaiting Gulfstream. The silver jet has the bold blue Carrington Steel logo proudly adorned on the tail. I shake my head still laughing at the recollection of me trading in my dad's old jet for my first Gulfstream which is now the oldest and one of many in the Carrington fleet.

I use the time in flight to review some of the global accounts for both Carrington Steel and Prestian Corp. I'm careful to copy Warren on my findings. He has accepted my previous role as COO for Prestian Corp. He's a smart man and learning fast. One more month of dual rolling and I'll feel completely comfortable turning over the reins to him. I look forward to the day that I can concentrate entirely on the global expansions of Carrington Steel.

In just under two hours we land at O'Hare and security escorts me to the helicopter that will drop me off at the top of my sky-rise overlooking Lake Michigan. The necessity of increased security is annoying. Paulie and Vitrie are with me as I open the rooftop door and get into the private elevator that will take me to my condo.

They are quiet until the doors close and we are away from the additional detail. "All the perimeters and your quarters have been cleared. Anything else you need?" Vitrie says as the door opens into my penthouse.

"That's it for now, but I may go out shortly," I say.

"You have any clue where so we can put some plans in place?" Paulie says.

I run my hand through my hair hating that I agreed to the added security on Chase's request. "I'd like to take in Millennial Park, maybe watch the parade and take a walk by the lake," I say gruffer than intended.

"No problem. We can make it happen. Just let us know when," Paulie says.

"Shit, I'm sorry, guys. I don't mean to be such an ass. It's Christmas," I say.

"No worries, Brian," Paulie says, slapping my back before he and Vitrie head back to the elevator and the doors close, leaving me on my own to brood. Paulie worked for my dad for eight years before he died and since then has worked for me. He's seen me at my worst on the holidays. He has no family left either and on more than one occasion he's been with me to see the holiday through.

I head to the kitchen and throw a K-Cup in the Keurig and

wait for it to brew. Even that leaves me filled with impatience. I shrug out of my suit jacket and throw it and my tie over the back of the dining room chair before firing up the Mac. Work never lets me down; it's a constant companion and source of comfort. I dig into a few of our overseas accounts and by the end of the morning I have operational structures in place to support a few of our expansions. I send them to the leaders of the steel mills and our corporate human resource department but glance up at my cell when a swoosh alerts me to an incoming message.

Message: Flight plans just registered for Prestian's jet. N.Y. to O'Hare, leaving in an hour.

Reply: Jenny?

Message: We're confirming, but most likely.

Reply: Keep me posted.

If she's leaving in an hour she'll be back in Chicago before evening with the time difference. *Why can't I get her out of my fucking head? Maybe because no one's ever turned you down or rejected you or tried to kick you in the fucking balls before!* Shit, maybe it's just been too long since I've been laid. A month since I broke it off with Sasha and almost two weeks since I hooked up with the voluptuous red-haired vixen in Italy. She looked so good but the sex was nothing I craved. It provided a necessary release and like most times left me feeling empty.

The thought saddens me and leaves me clamoring with pent up frustration. I know all I was looking for with Jenny was a quick hot fuck in a dark study on Christmas Eve. Maybe she had the right to kick me in the fucking balls. I could feel her desire pounding right through her heart, her hard little nipples straining against the flimsy material, poking me right in the chest and the way she moaned when I kissed her. God, she made my dick hard and I know she wanted me, too.

Message: They scrambled the flight plans. Jenny just boarded.

Reply: To Chicago?

Message: Not officially. Just got ground confirmation though. She's on the plane with Prestian security.

Reply: Thanks, Scottie. Let me know when she lands.

Message: Will do.

I sign into my Prestian account and clean up a few emails. There is nothing that Warren can't take care of or that needs my oversight. On the spur of the moment I decide that it's Christmas and we're going to fucking act like it is. I send Celia a text. While she's spending time with her family for the holidays she'll know exactly who to put me in touch with.

Message: Merry Christmas! Best caterer in town that I can persuade to do a last minute delivery?

Reply: Merry Christmas!! Elano's, they cater but also have walk in pick-ups and will put a nice meal together. Pay extra and have someone go get it. They are short staffed on the holiday!

Message: Will do, Celia! Thanks!

I instruct Siri to call Elano's, the first time I've felt back in control in over twelve hours. Damn that woman! As promised, if I have a driver pick it up we will have a twenty pound turkey, a spiral cut ham, mashed potatoes, gravy, rolls, sweet corn, and an assortment of pies.

Message: Paulie, can you have someone go get an order from Elano's? Then get your ass and entire crew up here at twelve noon. It's Christmas!

Reply: Can do on the pickup, can't leave the perimeter unsecure.

Message: I thought I was the boss.

Reply: I'm in charge of your safety. We'll split shifts.

Message: Make sure you spend time with all of your crew.

I change into a pair of jeans and a black t-shirt before the delivery and men start to arrive. Elano's has sent plates, utensils, napkins, and clear plastic glasses. The turkey comes encased on a black platter with a plastic covering. I remove the lid and eye it suspiciously as my security team laughs. Paulie brings one of the knives from the kitchen. "Move over, let the pro do this," he says, laughing as he begins to carve the turkey and the men continue to laugh.

"Fine, I'll take care of the potatoes," I say, taking a long silver spoon from the drawer and stirring them in the black container they arrived in.

Vitrie comes in with the last box of pies and sets them down on the counter. "How many friggin pies did you order?" he says, starting to line them up across the countertop.

I laugh as the men eye the apple, cherry, pumpkin, pecan, crème, and lemon meringue pies.

"You're a good man, Brian. When your mom was alive she

always had a huge gathering, lots of family, breakfast, followed by gifts and church service. Hard to believe it's been thirteen years," Paulie says.

"I know, after that Dad and I spent every Christmas morning having breakfast together. Neither of us was ready to do the whole family thing without her," I say.

"It rips my heart out that your father was taken from you. I wish to God I would have been on that team or that something would have been different that night, son," he says quietly while the other men are busy dishing themselves plates.

"Paulie, I don't blame the men that were on detail, I blame the reconnaissance team. They should have seen it coming, put plans in place, but they didn't. Something still feels off after all these years," I say.

"You're not wrong to feel that way, Brian. I've thought about it every single day since it happened and you're right. Someone was paid off, something got bent," he says, putting his arm around my shoulders.

The rest of the afternoon is spent talking and laughing with the crew and eating desserts. The loneliness has dissipated somewhat. These men are my family now and I vow never to have them out in the streets protecting me instead of celebrating the holidays again. Next year, I will make sure that wherever they are the ones they love are with them. They are packing up when I get the text from Scottie.

Message: Jenny's safe in her house and the place is secure.

Reply: She's alone at home?

Message: She's with Matt.

Reply: Who's Matt?

Message: The security detail Chase has assigned to her.

Reply: That Matt. Enjoy the rest of your holiday.

Message: They stopped by the liquor store for wine, lots of it.

Reply: It's Christmas.

Message: She's home alone except for Matt and he sure as shit better not be drinking.

Reply: What was the damage?

Message: Half a case and half a case to be delivered tomorrow.

Reply: What the fuck! Is she having a party?

Message: Something's troubling this girl.

Reply: Find out what the fuck it is then!

Message: We're on it.

I sigh heavily and sign into my laptop. I search the corporate contacts for Jenny's cell realizing that I've probably crossed some ethical corporate boundary. I enter her number into my phone and send her a text.

Message: Got your message yesterday. Are you with family today?

Reply: I spent time with them last week before the wedding.

Message: Christmas alone?

Reply: Kate and Chase flew out earlier today.

Message: If you're back in Chicago I can pick you up in about an hour. Show you Christmas in the city.

A half hour passes and she finally sends a note and I reread it a couple times before replying.

Message: I'm sorry for what I did. It's Xmas. Spend it with your loved ones.

Reply: I spent the afternoon with them. I'll pick you up shortly.

Message: No, you don't understand. I'm sorry. I just can't.

Reply: I'm not sure what happened, but you can't give up or wallow in remorse.

Message: I'm not sure what you think you know about me, but you don't have a fucking clue!

FIVE

JENNY

Matt follows me into the liquor store and he knows the drill by now, saying nothing as I put a selection of wines on the counter. He is one of the few people that know what happened that night, at least as much as anyone does. He doesn't judge me, but his jaw shifts when I pay for the six bottles they put into a carrying case and ask that they deliver the same amount to my house the next night. He takes the box from me and holds the door open with his back as I walk past him and the driver opens the door for us. "Anywhere else before we head home?" Matt asks.

I shake my head. "No, that'll do it tonight," I say, leaning back against the soft leather of the limousine Chase always has his driver chauffer Matt and me around in. It is useless to say no. Being Kate's best friend means I am stuck with her husband's controlling tendencies, especially when the family is dealing with Alfreita, the man who wants Chase dead. Alfreita will seize the opportunity to snatch anyone close to him or Kate to get at Chase.

When we get home, I run upstairs, shower, and slide into yoga pants, a sweater, and long boot socks with lace that I wear like 80's style leggings before heading downstairs. Matt has already settled himself in to watch the news in the living room.

"You want to sleep in the guest room?" I ask.

"Couch will do," he says offhanded. I've offered him the spare room time and time again when my niece isn't over, but he assures me that he likes my couch. I think he wants to be by the front door in case someone breaks in and it makes me glad that he's here.

I place Starbucks decaffeinated beans in the grinder and then start a fresh pot of coffee. As it brews, I pour a large glass of wine for myself. The night has started early. Just a few more things I need to do today, but no more people that I have to smile for... god the week has been exhausting. Smiling first for my family before the holidays even started and then with all of Jenny and Chase's family the last couple days. I take a sip of wine and then another as I watch the coffee slowly brew. The pot seems to take forever, dripping at its leisure. It's just one more thing to do before I can finally hide in my room and be anti-social. I slide the carafe out of the coffeemaker before it is quite done and pour a cup for Matt, placing a candy cane from the dish on the counter into the mug.

"Merry Christmas. I know you said it's not a thing, but I am really sorry that you're stuck here spending the holiday with me," I say, handing him the cup.

"Jenny, it's not a problem. Like I said, Chase and the security team are my family. I grew up in an orphanage," he says.

"Crap, I'm sorry, Matt. I didn't know that," I say.

"I don't share it with many people," he says, raising his cup in the air and toasting my wine glass. "Merry Christmas, Jenny," he says.

"If you want something to eat later your favorite pizza is in the freezer and there's some strawberry cheesecake and ice cream in there, too."

"Now what could be better than that on Christmas?" he says, smiling.

"Night, Matt. I'm heading up for the evening," I say, feeling his eyes on me as I take the bottle of wine along with my almost empty glass up the stairs.

I curl into bed and call my mom. It's the very last thing I have to do for anyone else tonight. I pour myself another glass of wine as the phone rings. She picks up after the third. "Merry Christmas, Honey," she says.

"Merry Christmas, Mom. How was your day?" I ask, knowing that I will be on the phone for at least another half hour. I sip my wine, starting to feel the tingling affects and relax enough to listen to her story about my niece and nephew waking up at the crack of dawn and dragging everyone downstairs to open gifts. I smile at the picture. My mom does a great job raising my older brother's kids after his wife abandoned them and he was injured in a motorcycle accident.

I fully intended to tell her what had happened to me while I was visiting, but seeing how much she has on her plate there was no way I could add to all of her angst and worry. I feel a pang of regret that I didn't have the plane fly me back to spend the holiday evening with her and the family, but it took every bit of my strength to get through the week at their house and act normal. Thank goodness for hard alcohol; small little vodka bottles that can be wrapped in clothes and emptied into glasses of coke or juice without anyone being the wiser.

We talk for a few more moments and disconnect before I hear the swoosh of my phone alerting me to an incoming message from Brian.

The offer to show me around the city is nice, but seems out of character. I briefly consider what it would be like strolling around Chicago with his hand holding mine, touching the back of my neck or kissing me again. I shake my head, recalling my erratic behavior. It's impossible. As if I needed a bigger indication than last night that I'm an emotional mess. Definitely not date material. I finally type a response and reread it several times before hitting the send button, surprised when his response is immediate.

Reply: I'm not sure what happened, but you can't give up or wallow in remorse.

Who the hell does he think he is? He has no clue what happened and no right to tell me I am wallowing. I might still be dealing with what happened but I get up every morning and put my big girl panties on, and do the work that needs to be done in order to make my father's inheritance into something he can be proud of. It's the only thing that allows me to send money home to my mother and family every week. Prick!

Message: I'm not sure what you think you know about me, but you don't have a fucking clue!

I pour myself another glass of wine. It must irk the hell out of him that I had the audacity not to go home with him last night and to turn down his offer. I've met rich arrogant men like that before but never one so forward. Just because he's the COO of a huge corporation gives him no right to speak to me like that.

I sip my glass of wine and settle in at my desk, glancing out the window at the snow lightly starting to fall. Winter in Chicago can be blustery and cold and this evening is no exception. I pull the sweater draped around my chair onto my shoulders and slip my arms inside its warmth.

I sign onto work email and in the next couple hours have all the human resource components of the expansion plans laid out. It's critical that we have that in place in anticipation of the rapid growth projections. I think back to what I could have lost in the last months with all of Ty's bullshit. Thank God Kate's overprotective boyfriend takes care of everyone that she cares about. I have a feeling now that I've agreed to dedicate a division of Torzial solely to Prestian Corp enterprises, once he and Kate return from their honeymoon things are going to become very fast paced.

I tip-toe downstairs and Matt is still watching television. The pot of decaffeinated coffee is mostly gone.

"I left you a couple pieces of pizza. They're on the stove. I thought you might get hungry," he says.

Damn it, he heard me. "Thanks, Matt," I say, placing the slices on a small plate and taking them and another bottle of wine upstairs. He knows me better than most people. I really am not sure how I'd manage without him. I can't even sleep in my own bed if he or my oldest niece isn't here, that's what a mess I am. She stayed with me for the last couple months, but is back with her mom now that school is on break for the holidays.

I sit back at my desk and scroll through Facebook, smiling at the pictures my sister has posted of her and my oldest niece with mom and the younger kids opening gifts this morning. My littlest niece is beautiful, adorned in a velvety red Christmas dress with white faux fur and my nephew is decked out in a handsome three piece suit. His chubby face is turned up in a scowl, tugging at his little tie and it's hard not to laugh. Do all males hate suits and ties?

It reminds my blurry mind of one man that looks absolutely amazing in a suit, a dark black one with a sapphire colored tie that is no rival to the deep sky-blue pools of his mesmerizing eyes. The way he took charge, dancing with me, powering me around the dance floor. I could feel the heat of his desire against my hipbone, urging me forward to the music, causing my nipples to harden beneath my dress, flaming the warmth between my legs. When he took me into the study I wanted him to kiss me. I wanted him to do a lot more than that. So what the hell happened? I know what the problem is I just can't talk about it. The counselor is probably more than a little frustrated with my tight lipped responses but the words just don't come.

I take a long pull of my wine remembering his comment about my wallowing. I decide to give him a piece of my mind, pulling up his last text. Someone should set that egotistical asshole straight and I determine that it will be me. I take another sip of wine. Wallowing? I can't even believe he would say such a thing. He doesn't even know me or what I've been through. I type out a message in my alcohol haze and reread the message before I hit the send button. There, take that you arrogant prick!

Message: For the record. You are an asshat!

I am surprised when within seconds I have a response to his message.

Reply: Whatever did I do to earn such an honor?

Message: You're arrogant, pompous and rude!

Reply: I think you have me all wrong, Ms. Torzial.

Message: I have you exactly correct, Mr. Carrington!

Reply: Details, I need corroborating evidence.

Message: You are forward!

Reply: Boring- You told me this last night. I admitted it. We should move on.

God this man makes my blood boil. Who the hell does he think he is? We did discuss it, but does he feel the need to throw it back in my face?

Message: Just another example of your arrogance and

forward behavior!

Reply: Please. I happen to know you liked my behavior.

I read his message three times before I can formulate a response. I blush, embarrassed. I did like his advances, the way he took charge, his kiss and the feel of his masculine heat against my body. Like hell he'll ever know that.

Message: Wow, your ego! What part of last night makes you believe that?

Reply: Perhaps your shallow breath, lovely blush or perky little nipples.

I take another sip of my wine.

Message: You think I wanted you?!?

Reply: Play coy all you want but we both know you did.

I'm not sure why I feel the need to goad him; maybe it's just the pure sarcastic arrogance that gets to me. Blame it on the alcohol. I do.

Message: Yes, clearly the night ended well.

I wait for a reply and when it is not forthcoming I return my attention to social media, flipping between my accounts, catching up on all the holiday posts. Skimming, watching all of my friends who seem so happy with their lives proudly displayed all over the screen. I take another sip and the knock on my door makes my head turn.

Matt is standing in the doorway with a bottle of wine and a plate of strawberry cheesecake. He holds up the bottle. "While I would definitely prefer that you not open this, I don't want you falling down the stairs trying to get to it," he says, setting it next to the second bottle on the desk, which is now only a fourth of the way full.

"Thanks, Matt. Sometimes I really don't know what I would do without you," I say, tears pooling in my eyes.

"Well it's a good thing you'll never have to find out. I'm not going anywhere, Jenny. Settle in for the night and promise to text me if you need anything else. I don't want you walking down those stairs," he says.

I sniff and grab a tissue from my desk. "I won't," I say.

"Good. I put the other three out of reach and canceled the delivery for tomorrow. If you want wine tomorrow, you'll make sure the other three bottles don't disappear tonight," he says.

"Matt!" I say, my cheeks getting hot with anger.

"Stop, I'm doing it for your own good. Finish what you have in the second bottle and go to sleep. If you need to, it's here, but we're going to have issues if you try to find the others. It's too much alcohol and my job is to protect you. If you continue down this path after the beginning of the New Year I'm going to talk to Chase and recommend rehab."

"Okay, just go," I say, knowing the drill and realizing I won't win.

I take a bite of the cheesecake and pour the remaining drops of bottle two into my glass. Still no word from Mr. Asshat. That will teach him for being so arrogant!

I take a few more bites of my cheesecake and manage to polish off the third bottle of wine while surfing through social media the rest of the night. I vaguely contemplate heading downstairs for another bottle but the thought of searching and dealing with Matt is too tiring. The alcohol has done its job. I lock the door and slip out of my clothes and underneath the covers, eventually drifting off to sleep.

I am looking into deep blue eyes and they hold me captivated with their intensity. I feel it before he begins to move, his mouth descending, devouring mine with his sensuous lips. Oh God, I open for him, his tongue finding mine, swirling, a dance only lovers know. He captures my bottom lip, pulling and sucking and then exploring my depths. I lean into him, all comprehensive thought is gone. His hands slide underneath my shirt cupping my breasts over the lace of my bra before unclasping it and caressing the sensitive exposed flesh between his fingers. My nipples continue to harden as the desire between my legs begins to pool. I gasp; my body is filled with longing. He reaches between my legs and begins to stroke me through the thin layer of clothing. I rise up, wanting him closer, needing to feel his heat. His fingers slip beneath the material, finding that special spot, caressing me, and I moan as he pushes against me, lightly at first, finding the rhythm and then stroking me as I feel myself climbing and climbing, the currents engulfing me, wave after incredible wave as I tremble around him.

I wake in a haze the next morning. In my hungover state, I vaguely recall what happened and tears begin rolling down my cheeks. It's the first time I've had an orgasm since before that fateful night, with my dreams always turning into violence and dousing the flames like a cold bucket of water.

SIX

BRIAN

I read her text for the twentieth time tonight and always come back to the same thing.

Message: Yes, clearly the night ended well.

She's angry with me for being forward. I get that, but she wanted me as much as I wanted her; everything in her body's response told me that. The little hitches in her breath, her widened eyes, the pulse throbbing on the side of her neck, the hardened nipples that were driving into my chest and the heat of her body as it pressed against me. Why is she so angry with me? Why if she wanted me so much did she push me away and try to kick me in the balls? I read Scottie's report and my mind conjures up the possible reasons but I push them down, wanting with every fiber of my being to think that what I'm assuming is not true. I send a message to Scottie.

Message: I need all the details ASAP!

Reply: You should have them in your inbox by the time you wake up.

Message: Send what you have now.

Reply: No can do. Couple pieces of intel coming in that need to be included.

Message: Shit! You know I hate waiting.

Reply: I need to be sure. In the a.m. It's Xmas!

I pour back the scotch I've been drinking. Only Scottie can get away with this. He's been with our family for years.

I t is barely four a.m. when I pull on jogging pants, socks, and my running shoes before heading to the kitchen. I place a K-Cup in the machine, waiting for it to brew.

"Jesus! Does it always need to take so long to get a cup of coffee?" I exclaim, but no one is there to hear me. Celia won't be coming back until tomorrow. I grab my coffee and drink a little of it on the way to the lower level. The elevator opens and I scan the custom designed gym. I typically hit the treadmill first, but today, I need an overpowering release. I take another swig of coffee and put my cup down, donning the black boxing gloves in the corner of the room and warily eye the long red bag hanging from the ceiling that I have not used in ages.

The first blow is hard, I intend to do it damage, but it mocks me, swinging back. I hit it again, but not hard enough and it comes back at me taunting. I do it again, and again, and again, pounding it, until after an hour of heavy exertion my body is pouring sweat and I am exhausted. I head into the adjacent room and strip, walking into the stone shower and under the multiple showerheads. I wash my hair and let the soap and rinse water continue to rain down on my body. While I may have calmed emotionally my body still remembers her scent, the way she felt in my arms, the way she kissed and tasted. My cock is on fire, pulsing and raging and in just a matter of moments and strokes of my own hand my load is shooting all over the walls of my highly-priced designer shower. I lean my heated forehead against the cool tiles, watching as the evidence of my desire swirls down the drains. Jesus, when was the last time I jacked off like that?

I put on a pair of jeans and a long sleeve henley before heading to the kitchen to make myself another cup of coffee. The swishing of my phone alerts me to an incoming text from Scottie.

Message: Docs in your inbox.

Reply: Thx.

I open the email. What is she hiding, what's her story? Why is it so important for me to know? I can't get her out of my head because she's the first woman that's pushed me away, not wanted my advances, damn—kicked me in the balls she was so serious about it! Am I really that arrogant? Her texts from the last night rewind over and over. Pompous and arrogant, oh, and let's not forget a total asshat!

I skim through the cover and introductory sheets, already

acquainted with her name, place of employment, address of residence and age. I go through the documents looking for things Scottie didn't already update me on or that I don't already know, but nothing tells me what happened to make the light go out of those beautiful green eyes when she's in the throes of passion and then remembers something that scares the shit out of her.

* * *

It's a little over a week later on Monday morning. I am in my Chicago office when Chase calls. "Welcome back. Have a good trip?" I ask, pulling my eyes and attention from the productivity reports.

"I don't think the honeymoon could have been better," he says.

"Good to hear. You back in the office?" I ask.

"Alfreita is still an issue. Jay has us working from home this week. Good news is that everything's right on schedule for the grand opening in L.A. Friday evening."

I groan inwardly, recalling the invitation. Listening to a bunch of investors does not sound like fun to me. I usually leave that to Chase and make a mental note to send a message of apology later in the week. "I'm sure the community will be out in full swing. They really need to build the city's infrastructure and this should help," I say.

"Yeah, about that, I purchased land just north of there, closer to the Carrington sky-rise. The current facility will suffice for a year and give Torzial exposure on the west coast. I told Jenny and Katarina that I'll be building another Prestian Corp Tower within the year and then Jenny will purchase the sky-rise from me. They're both planning to be there Friday night to talk with investors about the Torzial expansion plans," Chase says.

"That's insightful," I say, tuning back in at the mention of Jenny.

"Are you planning to attend?"

"I'll be there," I say before my brain can catch up with my mouth.

"Excellent."

"The Carrington board meeting is the day before so I'll probably spend the end of the week in the area," I say, even though not days ago I would have been on the first plane back to Chicago or New York after the meeting. What the hell is wrong with me?

"How's everything transitioning for Warren?" Chase says.

"Your new COO is more than ready to take my place here at Prestian Corp. There hasn't been much to oversee or intervene in. As far as I'm concerned he's handling everything great. In fact, I might want to persuade him to work for me at Carrington Steel," I say, smirking.

Chase laughs out loud. "Well that's an excellent sign of endorsement coming from you. Let me know if you need anything, otherwise I'll plan to see you at the end of the week. Right now we're planning to fly out Friday afternoon."

"See you then," I say, typing Torzial Consulting into Google search. Her picture comes up. Long silky smooth brunette hair that I've felt against my neck dancing, those deep green eyes, ones you can drown in. That mouth that feels like warm honey wrapped around my lips and against my tongue, opening for me, drawing me in before she kicks me in the balls or strikes out with that sharp little tongue of hers. I glance down at the message still on my phone.

Message: Yes, clearly the night ended well.

I don't know if I'd like to fuck her or spank the shit out of her sassy little ass until she screams. Maybe I should spank her and then fuck her. Maybe that would get her out of my system. I text Scottie to let him know there's been a change in plans and that I'll be staying at my condo in L.A. Thursday night before I email my assistant to have her switch all my meetings to virtual on Friday. I take a look at Jenny's profile one more time and then read Scottie's reply.

Message: FYI –Jenny Torzial is moving into the old Bell-stone sky-rise.

I hit his contact and he answers on the first ring. "What's going on? That wasn't in the report," I say.

"No lad. She just signed papers right before Christmas and closes at the end of January, but looks like she'll be leasing until then since the property is vacant."

My cock twitches at the thought that she'll be closer to me and I shift to adjust trying to focus on what Scottie's saying. "She hired a company to move all of her stuff at the end of the week into the condo and a painting company and flooring outfit are scheduled to go into the house and do some work the very next day," he says.

Jenny Torzial. I've seen that sharp mind at work more than a few times in email exchanges I've been copied on related to her company's work on behalf of Prestian Corp. It doesn't take her long to make a decision and once she does things move fast.

SEVEN

JENNY

L.A. is sunny and when Matt and I land a limo is waiting to take us to the newly purchased building that will be rebranded as the Prestian Towers. "It's going to be a reality check once there's no longer a need for security and Chase quits flying me around in jets and having you escort me in limousines," I say, sliding into the back seat of a long sleek black limo before Matt gets in across from me.

"Yeah, the boss knows how to travel in style, that's for damn sure," he says, grinning.

The driver has the air conditioning on and I go to push the button to open the window and let the fresh air in. Matt reaches it first, shaking his head. "Security precaution, only I do that," he says.

"Seriously?" I say, narrowing my eyes at him.

"Afraid so, Jay's a stickler on protocol. I can have the driver turn the ac down if it's too cool," he says.

"No, its fine," I say, wondering how long all of the high level security will continue.

The limo pulls up to the sleek chrome sky-rise that towers above the others and as we step out and look up at the building I feel my heart racing. In one year I will buy this glass and chrome structure from Chase and at that time it will become the Torzial sky-rise. I hold back a tear of remorse that my father isn't alive to see this. A small amount of his life insurance was my inheritance and what I used for the start-up of Torzial Consulting. Never in my wildest dreams did I believe that I would ever have my own sky-rise, but thanks to Chase it's a possibility. He was able to buy this at such a low price that in one year he will sell it to me and move into his new Prestian Corp towers. I will then take over ownership and Torzial will have a sky-rise of it's own in Los Angeles.

Security escorts us into the impressive foyer. The red carpet trails into the magnificent stone floors of the lobby. The twinkling crystal chandeliers hang from the vaulted ceilings and the rich cherry wood of the reception area is polished to a high sheen. We walk through the striking reception area towards the conference center where most of the meetings are scheduled throughout the course of the day.

It's almost four p.m. by the time I open the door to the Torzial suite, another of Chase's surprises, which is located one floor directly beneath the Prestian Penthouse. I glance around and take in the opulence. The windows allow an impressive view of the Los Angeles city-scape for miles. The living area is decidedly contemporary. A pure white couch with an extended chaise and matching ottoman are situated in the middle of the room with chrome and glass furniture placed here and there. A mink-looking throw is lying over the back of the sofa adding the only bit of warmth to the otherwise stark room. The fireplace is encased in blue/black slate marble and there is a sleek black television monitor overhead. I look forward to adding my own belongings and creating a little warmth to the space.

The kitchen resembles the same bluish/black slate as the fireplace with white cupboards and chrome lighting. There is a Sub-Zero refrigerator and stainless steel wine refrigerator. I'm sure I'll enjoy that later, but right now I need a shower. I pull my hair up so it doesn't get wet and then slip under the raining warmth of the silky feeling drops to wash away the day's travels. After applying a little moisturizer to my damp skin, I decide there's just enough time for a nap before the event.

The alarm rouses me after an hour. I style my hair adding a few curls and gathering it to one side with a sparkly slide, allowing the wavy tresses to fall over my breasts before slipping into the long mint colored gown Chase's shopper selected for me. Saying no to the generous offer of a personal shopper to select our dresses for the grand opening gala was something that neither Kate nor I could do. My dress is low cut but not to excess and cinches at the waist before flowing around me and I couldn't be more pleased with the choice.

The tours of the facility are just starting as I arrive downstairs and the next couple hours are spent talking with potential lessees of the building and community members. The last group is almost finished about twenty minutes before the ribbon cutting ceremony begins when I glance down at the message from Kate.

Message: Chase and I are here. Where are you?

Reply: Still with the tour group. Back to first floor shortly.

When I arrive downstairs, waiters and waitresses are carrying large silver trays, handing out champagne in fluted glasses to the throng of guests. I take one for myself and weave my way among the crowd to the reserved table in the front of the conference room where I see Kate.

She is wearing a midnight blue ball gown with delicate straps and when she turns to take a seat I notice the back is completely bare. She has the diamond necklace and silver bangles on that Chase gave her and they complement the dress perfectly. She smiles widely as I approach and lean down to give her a quick hug before taking the seat next to her. "It's going to be such a fun few days! I'm anxious to hear all about your honeymoon and excited that we'll have the weekend to catch up," I say, taking a sip of my drink.

"It was everything I could have dreamed of and better," she says, looking across the room at her husband who is talking with the city mayor.

"Yeah, well while you were off gallivanting around the Caribbean islands on a yacht I was slaving away, trying to get

Torzial all moved into the Prestian Corp towers and guess what else?" I say.

"Give me a clue?" she says, smiling at me over her wine glass.

"I bought a condo!"

"Congratulations! Where is it and when can I see it?" she says.

"It's not too far from Prestian Corp. I was trying to get as close as I could but some of the others were a little more than I wanted to spend. Still within walking distance when the weather is nice though," I say.

"That's great! I didn't even know you were considering selling your house," she says.

"Actually, I'm having it updated a bit and then I'm going to rent it to my niece and her boyfriend. They've been looking for a place together and it's not far from his work or her school. Plus with Torzial moving into Prestian Corp the drive just doesn't make sense anymore."

"I am so excited for you and for us! We can do so much more together now," she says as Chase slips into the seat next to her and puts his arm around her shoulders.

"Nice to see you again, Jenny," he says to me.

"Likewise, Chase. I can't believe this will actually be the Torzial sky-rise next year. Things on the work front are moving so fast," I say.

"Speaking of moving. Jenny just bought a condo not too far from Prestian Corp," she says.

He raises his eyebrows. "Which building?" he says.

"The old Bellstone property. The space has been vacant for a while so I was able to get it for a great price. Not only that, but they let me lease until the official closing. Actually, all my personal belongings are being moved today and I hired Sara's company to unpack for me over the weekend. She's expanding her services from just cleaning to a variety of other things," I say.

"Congratulations, that's in a great area and will save you commute time," he says.

"Thanks. I can't wait to get settled in," I say, just as the mayor is announced and begins talking about the city's revitalization plan.

Chase is introduced next and he heads to the stage and takes the mic, seemingly at ease with talking in front of large crowds, sharing the Prestian Corp vision and how being a part of the Los Angeles community fits into the long-term goals of the organization.

My name is called and I try to swallow my nerves. "Don't be anxious. You look absolutely amazing and I'm so excited for you," Kate says, squeezing my hand. The extra little bit of encouragement helps and I join the group on the way up to the stage. The crowd erupts into large cheers when we're finished and I can't help the feeling of pride at being part of such a huge community project.

I stop by our table briefly to let Kate know I'm joining the last tour for the evening and will text her when I'm done. "Okay, join us for drinks when you're finished," she says.

"Sounds good," I say, taking a sip of champagne before hurrying to find the last of the tour group.

One of the new renters is accompanied by his wife, a designer for many of Hollywood's elite. She is eagerly talking about decorating ideas for the floor he intends to lease as we're led through the facility. After an hour of showing the spaces the team decides to head up to see the rooftop pool. I say good night to everyone having already seen it, pressing the button for the main floor. The elevator door closes behind me as I step out of it and when I look up, the man standing in front of me robs every breath from my body.

EIGHT

BRIAN

The last meeting of the day runs longer than anticipated and I tap out a text to let Chase know I'll be late. My driver, Wes, navigates the Friday evening traffic skillfully and we're soon pulling up to the temporary Prestian headquarters that next year will be Jenny's.

I walk into the foyer and round the corner looking for signage that will take me to the floor where the event is being held. As I reach the elevator the sight in front of me sends my body into a rage. I recognize Jenny's hair and face. She's backed up against the elevator, her hands on a man's chest. She is white as a ghost and trembling against the wall.

I stalk forward grabbing him by the neck and just seeing the fear in her wide open green eyes makes my grip tighten before security begins closing in. "I don't think the lady is interested," I say, spinning him around. Ty. I immediately recognize him from the profiles Scottie sent over last week. "Get him the fuck out of here before I kill him," I roar, throwing him towards Matt's team.

Jenny hasn't said a word; she's just looking straight ahead as he's hauled off but then all of a sudden gags and pushes past me, making her way to the ladies room.

"How did that asshole get within a foot of her?" I snarl at one of the security men.

"I saw him talking to her. It didn't look suspicious at first, but as soon as he stepped closer and she backed up we started moving in," the younger guy says.

"Save it," I say as I see Matt, the man who's been put on point for her security. I grab him by the shirt. "How the fuck did he get this close to her? She's in there retching her guts out. How did he get past the detail?"

He grabs me by the wrist and I loosen my hold on his shirt. "No excuses here. It's on me. We've got a new guy with us. I was getting orders for the night from Jay and had him watch her," he says, speaking of the man who is now across the room talking with the other security guards. "I would have recognized that son of a bitch in a heartbeat," he says, clearly as pissed with himself as I am with him.

Jenny comes out of the restroom still staring straight ahead before making a beeline for the open elevator doors. I close the distance in a few large strides, placing my hand on the door, watching her, waiting for Matt and the dipshit with him to get in before allowing the door to close behind us.

She's eerily quiet. "Jenny, he's not here anymore. He's been escorted off the premises and security has been doubled. By now they all have his picture and won't allow him onto the property," Matt says.

She doesn't respond. Shit, she looks shell shocked. I tilt her chin, forcing her eyes upward, but there's nothing going on behind those deep green eyes, just nothing. The elevator opens and she walks right out, doesn't say a word, just swipes her private card into the scanning device. The green light comes on and she enters her room, closing the door behind her.

NINE

JENNY

I **can't get it out of my head**... Every ten minutes my mind just keeps replaying the same scenario, over and over.

"Hello, Jenny," he says. The blond hair and squinting eyes purposely take in every inch of my body, bold, as if he's trying to undress me and it makes my blood run cold. He comes closer and I can't move, completely immobilized except for the uncontrollable trembling, every instinct telling me to scream or do something but my body doesn't listen.

"I keep thinking about the last time we were together, how much I liked it, how good you looked that night," he says, smiling maliciously.

"Soon Jenny, very soon," he says, his lips a millimeter away from mine, upturned into an evil smirk. My neurons finally engage and I push against him. A moment later a head of stark black hair appears and suddenly there are strong hands around Ty's throat and he's lifted and pulled away from me.

"I don't think the lady is interested," Brian says. The hands that only two weeks ago were caressing my own neck are now holding Ty in a death grip. He is struggling to get air, desperately clawing at the hands so close to squeezing the life out of him. "Get him the fuck out of here before I kill him," Brian says, throwing Ty towards Matt's team as they arrive.

A wave of nausea suddenly overtakes me and I stumble past Brian, gagging, barely making it into an open stall in the women's bathroom before heaving the contents of my stomach, retching again and again. I am still kneeling on the bathroom floor when it finally subsides and the flushing of the toilet finally produces clear water. I know I can't stay here, it's not safe. He will find me. Self-preservation kicks in and I race to the elevator and Brian, Matt and some other guy get in with me. I hear the words coming out of Matt's mouth but can't respond. Nothing comes out. The elevator dings and I walk straight ahead, swiping my card in the door and closing it behind me. I am frantically pulling clothes out of my suitcase when my phone vibrates and I look at the message from Kate.

TEN

BRIAN

I watch her as she closes the door behind her and damn if I don't feel like a helpless fuck.

"Let's go find Jay," I say to Matt. "You think you can handle keeping her secure now that she's behind a locked door?" I ask his sidekick.

Matt gives me a glare, as though I should feel remorse for the man whose cheeks have reddened at my outburst. I don't fucking care about his feelings. I still don't know exactly what happened to Jenny but after tonight I do know whatever he did was something horrible.

I text Chase letting him know that I need to talk with him and to meet me in the conference room ASAP. We get downstairs and I look around not seeing him yet and order a scotch on the rocks. I send another message.

Message: We need to talk now!

What the hell is taking him so long? He arrives moments later with Kate on his arm and looks up scowling at me as I down the last of my drink. He whispers something into her ear and nods to me from across the room. She takes a seat by Chase's dad and his girlfriend as Chase makes his way over to me.

"Ty was here. That son of a bitch had Jenny cornered next to the elevator and your pathetic security men stood there and let it happen," I say, not caring that Matt is standing next to me.

Chase levels his gaze on me. "What exactly happened?"

"I don't know. He was in her face and she was white, absolutely terrified, just fucking standing there, shell shocked. She had her hands on his chest trying to push him away and I got him by the back of the neck before he could put his slimy mouth on her," I say, knowing that if I had been one second later he would have.

"Damn it! Matt can you give Jay an update and let's see what we can do to get to the bottom of this," Chase says, heading back to the table where he has left Kate and Don, leaving me no choice but to follow in his wake.

Chase's dad cuts to the point right away. "What's going on son?"

"Ty was here. He cornered Jenny and Brian intervened," Chase says.

"What happened, Brian?" Kate says, putting her drink down.

I don't want to sit here and answer questions but the pained look in the eyes of Jenny's best friend softens me a bit. "When I got here he was in her face by the elevator and I could tell whatever he said shook her pretty bad. The security team must have realized something was happening about the same time I did. I intervened and had security throw him out," I say, leaving out the part about their fuck up and my almost choking the life out of him.

"Oh, my God. I need to be with Jenny. Where did she go?" Kate asks.

"She's in the Torzial suite. It's one floor below ours," Chase says and Kate begins rapidly texting.

She looks down at her phone when she hears a swooshing sound and shakes her head. "She wants to be alone," she says, tapping another message into her phone.

"She'll be fine, Kate. We've got security watching her and I'm heading back up and won't leave my post outside of her door all night," Matt says.

"Dad, if you're going to hang and mingle for a little while longer, I'll take Kate upstairs to get some well needed rest," Chase says.

"Of course, son. We've got this," Don says.

"Brian, there are a few open suites. One of them is just below the Torzial suites floor. I'll have Jay give you a key if you don't want to drive across town in this traffic," Chase says.

I would much rather be in the penthouse of the Carrington sky-rise but I decide to stay. "I just may take you up on that," I say, pocketing the master key that Jay holds out for me. They leave and I wander over to the open bar, order another scotch on the rocks and down it before heading to the Torzial floor. The elevator opens and there are two doors on the floor. True to his word Matt is outside of her suite. Satisfied, I flip the magnetic strip over in my hand and head back to the elevator and floor below to my own suite, swiping the key card Jay provided. The space seems decent enough. Nothing fancy, but it will do. I lay my jacket and tie over a kitchen chair before sending a message to Wes with instructions to deliver an overnight bag and clothes for morning. Certainly not the evening I had planned when I got here.

I pick up the phone and hit Scottie's contact. He answers on the first ring. "I need in-depth info on that bastard right away," I say, proceeding to fill him in on the details of the evening.

"Brian, we don't have all the information, yet. He's apparently had a few skirmishes with women over the years. He was accused of a few assault and battery charges but they never resulted in anything more than a slap on the wrist."

"Keep me posted," I say, disgruntled.

I wake up feeling less than refreshed. I blame the unfamiliar surroundings on my restlessness and not the white trembling little body I left last night. I decide to check on her before meeting with Chase. I take the stairs one floor up and Matt greets me as I reach the Torzial floor. "Where's your friend?" I say.

"He's no longer on her detail. I sent him home," he says.

I nod, knocking on her door. No answer. "Do you have a key?" I say.

"I do, but need to confer with Jay before we intrude on her privacy," Matt says.

"Fuck that, I'll talk to him," I say, storming into the elevator and entering the code Chase gave me for the Prestian suites.

The elevator opens right into the massive penthouse. Well this is more like it. "Morning," Chase and Jay say, almost in unison.

"Brian, I know why you're here. I'm sending the team in to check on her right now," Jay says, busy on his phone and it's obvious that Matt's already apprised him of the situation.

"Good, she may just be asleep but if she's still looking the same way she did last night I'm having a physician stop by and take a look at her," I say, ignoring Chase's raised eyebrows and Kate's head turn to look at me.

"Chase, they just went in. No sign of Jenny anywhere," Jay says, immediately texting a message into his phone.

"Fuck, how the hell is it that a hundred pound woman slips through your security detail?" I yell, running my hands through my hair.

"Calm the fuck down, Brian. This isn't helping anyone," Chase says and I know he's right but that doesn't prevent me from wanting to punch Matt right in the mouth. He was there all night; his only job was to keep her safe.

Kate's face turns ash white. "We have to find her," she says and her voice is barely above a whisper.

Chase pulls her into his arms holding her tight. "We'll find her Baby," he says, kissing the top of her head.

Jay disconnects from his phone call and begins summarizing the situation for everyone. "Two possibilities at this point. She somehow got by our security during the time we were putting plans in place or went out the alternative safe escape during the night, which I don't believe is possible. We've had a guard stationed outside both areas all night long," Jay says.

"What's the third alternative?" Kate asks and I see Chase's arm instinctively tighten around her.

"We know Alfreita's men are in the city. Let's hope he isn't involved," he says.

"Chase, what if he has her? We have to find her fast. You know what will happen to her if we don't," she says and I don't fucking like the way that sounds at all.

"We'll find her, Baby," Chase says, wiping the tears that have begun falling down her face.

"The helicopter will be here in less than twenty minutes to take you to the airstrip. I want everyone up in the air as quickly as possible."

"I can't leave without Jenny," Kate protests.

"Excuse us gentlemen. Katarina and I will return shortly," Chase says, guiding his wife into their master bedroom.

Alfreita held Kate's mom hostage earlier in the year and Chase has said that he will stop at nothing to get what he wants but that's all the information I have. I need to know what the plan is to find Jenny and right the hell now, but Jay accepts another incoming call on his cell. I take the moment to glare at him, but he doesn't seem phased and keeps talking.

Chase and Kate come out of the bedroom and she looks solemn. "We're all packed and ready to go," he says, although Kate appears tight lipped. She looks pissed but Chase is right to get her the hell out of here.

"If you'll excuse me, I need to take care of a few things. I'll let you know when the helicopter lands," Jay says, walking to the elevator.

"Hold up, I'm coming with you," I say, following him.

"Fine," he says, as I get onto the elevator with him and Matt.

"What's the plan?" I ask.

"My men are setting up a temporary communication and intel station in one of the spare suites. Our main teams are focused on finding Alfreita and getting a communication lock. I didn't want to say too much in front of Kate, but if Alfreita took her, we need information on every aerial flight, helicopter, jet, and ocean cruiser that's been in the air or ported out to sea in the last twelve hours. My men are working on following a path to every single one of them. Last year he kidnapped Kate's mom. When he took Karissa, his intent was to dump her into the human trafficking trade after he got what he wanted from Chase. We need to find her fast," he says.

I am internally seething, ready to fucking explode, but outwardly the only indication is the slight twitch to my jaw. "I'll have Scottie send in more of my men to help. We have overseas connections that may be valuable in case that's what happened," I say, sending Scottie a text message.

"I'll take you up on the offer of men, we can use more boots on the ground, but the intel team we have is bar none," he says.

"They'll be joining you," I say, matching his steely grey eyes.

He nods. "I want their profiles along with all aliases, current level of clearances, and they go through the same background screening we require for anyone else we bring on board," Jay says.

I nod. I wouldn't expect anything less from my own head of security. Although Jay's new employee totally fucked up, I know Chase trusts Jay and he's saved his life and that of Kate's on more than one occasion. "I can respect that," I say, nodding before tapping out a message to send the requested information to the secure mail account Jay provides.

I am impressed that in under an hour the entire intel operation is set up and at the efficiency with which my team members are cleared and put in the air. All the existing details are given assignments of running credit card traces on buses, trains, cabs, rent-a-cars, and airplane logs along with cruise ships and commercial carriers searching for one sliver of a clue that will allow us to trail her. It is only mid-afternoon and already I feel exhausted with the feeling of defeat and despair. How does someone just vanish into the fucking air?

My team arrives and I spend time greeting them as they are

quickly brought up to speed on the different modes of transportation coming into and out of the city the previous night and additional assignments are doled out.

Jay and Matt are talking in lowered voices in the corner but at the mention of Ty's name I join them. "What's the plan?" I demand.

Jay sighs. "If you want to hang out here and be available to the team we're going to take another crew and pay Ty a visit. Nose around a bit," Jay says.

"Pay someone else to babysit. I'm coming with you," I say. There's no fucking way they're keeping me from going.

We ring the doorbell and Ty answers it. "What can I do for you?" he says. The blackened eye and busted lip he's sporting gain Jay's security team a little bit of my respect. There's bruising around his neck from the damage that I did but clearly he received another message when they escorted him off the premises. The cocksucker is standing there cool and collected and the upturned smile on his face makes me regret not having squeezed harder last night. If he has her, I'll kill him with my bare hands.

"We'd like to discuss Jenny," Jay says.

"What about her? She's a whore that I spent some time with earlier in the year. We haven't seen each other for a while but I think she wants a redo," he says, smirking at us.

I lash out, grabbing him by the throat, squeezing hard, envisioning him sucking his last breath of air but Jay's hands are strong, unlocking the death grip I have on the fucker's throat.

"She's missing you son of a bitch and you're the primary suspect," I say.

He looks genuinely shocked by that and I can't tell if he's just a great actor or if the surprise is real. "You think I had something to do with it? Look, there's no love lost between us, but I have nothing to hide. Come on in, take a look around," he says.

"Don't mind if we do," Jay says, signaling with a nod for security to follow us and for the backup around the perimeter to be on alert.

"We walk in and Jay and Matt have him covered at all times as he leads us through his house. We have gone through every room and are leaving before he says anything else. "Too bad she's missing, I was looking forward to having some fun with the little whore while she was in town," he says.

I turn around and the next thing I know my fist is connecting with his teeth and blood is spewing across his cream colored walls and stone floors. He cries out in pain. "You broke my fucking teeth you psycho bastard."

I move closer, willing myself to remain in check. "I get a report that you've come within fifty feet of that woman and I'll do more than that. They'll find your fucking body floating in the goddamn bay," I say, spinning on one heel and walking right out the door.

It's much later in the day and I've just showered after a run on the coast, needing time away after an afternoon spent listening to the commotion in the communications station with no fucking progress. My phone vibrates and I hit the accept button seeing Chase's name flash on the screen.

"Brian here," I say.

"We just got home. Jay told me what happened at Ty's house. I didn't want to say too much in front of Katarina earlier but Ty brutally raped her. I won't go into detail but leave it to suffice that seeing him in person was probably more than she could take. You have to believe our teams are doing everything they can to find her."

I had already come to the conclusion that may have been what happened but hearing it confirmed leaves my mouth dry. "Everything they can isn't enough. If you haven't noticed she's still fucking missing and no one knows how or why," I say.

"We know how. When the new guard was outside her door and you and Matt were filling me in downstairs he left his post. Matt feels horrible; he thinks the world of Jenny. He's been assigned as her security detail since the rape."

"Fucking incompetence. I want an hour-by-hour update!"

"Brian, ease up a bit. Give them space to do their job and stay away from Ty. Let the security teams handle him," Chase says.

"I'll wring the life right out of him if I ever see the fucker again," I say.

"Listen, I wanted to give you a little background since I couldn't this morning, but the real reason I'm calling is that they got a lead while you were out," he says.

"What was it?"

"A taxicab driver picked a young woman up outside of Prestian Towers with long dark hair. It was in a ponytail and she was wearing an Adidas zip up jacket. That's all he could remember from the rearview mirror but he thought it was odd since everyone else around the sky-rise was dressed up for the grand opening. He worked the night shift and just got back on duty an hour or so ago."

"Where did he drop her?" I ask.

"Here's where it gets a little strange. She asked him to drive her around and show her the city. He gets requests like that all the time so didn't think too much of it but she wasn't paying any attention to him as he pointed out attractions. She just had this blank look on her face and when he asked her where she wanted to go after about an hour, she told him to take her back to Prestian Towers," he says.

"What the hell."

"I just received a message from Jay that they're starting a search of all the open suites in the building and every vacant room within the block. It's possible she doubled back," Chase says, but that's all I need to hear. I am out the door, bypassing the elevators to sprint the one floor up to the intel room.

"Chase told me the plan. You have an order of how the area gets searched?" I say, bursting into the room as the team looks up at me.

Jay nods, pulling up the spreadsheet with assignments on his phone to show me. "In less than twenty minutes all rooms will have been searched according to this grid," he says.

Okay, now I'm getting some respect for this security team. "Send a copy to my phone. I'll come with you, Matt," I say.

"We've got the top floors down. She's not in the penthouse, the Torzial floor is her room and the intel area you're standing in has been checked," he says as we get on the elevator to the floor below us. "There are two suites on this floor," he says.

"I slept in the one to the right last night," I say.

"All suites get searched. Left first and then that one second," Matt says, letting me know in no uncertain terms that mine's no exception to his search before rapping on the door and swiping the master across the detector. "According to our floor plan, both are vacant until the owners take occupancy," he says, waving the key card until it registers green.

He pushes the door open and there is a loud clatter as something falls to the floor. "The door is blocked," he says, unholstering his gun as we push past it and enter the room. I bump into him as he stops dead in his tracks. "Son of a bitch," I say under my breath.

She is sitting upright in bed, green eyes wide open and staring straight ahead, just like the taxicab driver described. Her long brown hair is in a ponytail and she is still wearing the black Adidas jacket. Her knees are bent and she is leaning on them.

Matt hits a button on his phone and says quietly, "We've got her Jay. She's a floor down from Torzial in one of the spare rooms." I walk around him and tilt her chin. Again with the empty stare.

"Come on, you're going home, Jenny," I say, ignoring

Matt's glare as I slip my arms around her back and under her knees. Her arms instinctively wrap around me and it feels as though she has a death grip on my neck. Something in my heart constricts as I carry her out of the room and to her own suite. Matt unlocks her door and holds it open so I can place her on the couch in the middle of the room. Her grip tightens around my neck as I try to set her down. Fuck it. I hold her in my lap until Jay walks in.

"Brian, Alfreita's men are swarming the entire town. We need a plan to get you both up in the air and her safely to the Prestian estates," Jay says.

"I'll take her," I say, and catch a little flicker in her eye. It's just barely something, so brief I might have imagined it.

"I was hoping you would say that. Matt and his team can return with you and I'll be able to keep extra men here if you go together," Jay says before connecting on his cell to give instructions about the logistics.

In less than half an hour I am carrying Jenny onto the awaiting Augusta. It is one of the fastest moving helicopters in the world and one of three in the Prestian Corp fleet. "This baby will get you to the private strip outside of LAX faster than any other chopper in the world and we'll have a jet waiting that will take you to Chicago," Jay says as we climb aboard.

"Good, let's get in the air as quick as we can," I say, trying to get a handle on my emotions. I buckle her in and she stays pressed against me the entire trip.

"Damn that thing can move," I say to Jay as I carry Jenny to the jet. This beautiful woman, broken and sad, is still grasping my neck like it's the only lifeline she has. I lay Jenny on the sectional in front of the fireplace that is already emitting warmth throughout the cabin of the Gulfstream. Matt opens one of the overhead bins and pulls out a pillow and blanket handing them to me.

"Thanks, Matt," I say, tucking her into the comfort of the blankets. "You're safe, we're all with you. Sleep, Sweetheart," I say, pushing the long strands of brunette curls out of her eyes. She grasps my hand securing it like a vice, not letting go and clearly not going to fall asleep easily. I lift her into the air and slide onto the couch pulling her beside me before placing the blankets over the top of us.

Her head nestles onto my chest and her hand tightens on mine. Her eyes are wide open, wary, but nothing else is going on. She just stares at the fireplace until she eventually drifts to sleep. A call to the Carrington physicians will assure she's looked at as soon as we touch down and I make a note to have her therapist contacted. An hour later I'm starting to doze myself and her whole body suddenly jerks and she gasps, deep green eyes wide and alert, now turning her head to look at me. "Easy, you're safe Sweetheart."

ELEVEN

JENNY

Ty wants to hurt me again. I remember his face, his grin by the elevator and Brian dragging him off of me and then just needing to escape. The night is all coming back, and with it the incredible fear and need to move quickly. He can figure out which room I'm in. I shimmy out of my dress and pull on a pair of yoga pants along with my Adidas jacket, gathering my hair into a ponytail. I hear the distant ping of the elevator and my blood runs cold. There are only two suites on this floor and the other is vacant. I race out the door to find security before whoever gets off the elevator can reach me but no one is there. I am completely alone.

Fear and adrenaline course through my veins and I duck into the stairwell, running as fast as I can down the steps to the floor below, riding the elevator to the main lobby. I join the group in front of me as we make our way through the crowded reception area, past the doorman and onto the street outside. I walk a short distance from the sky-rise to one of the taxis parked at the curb, open the back door and get in.

"Where to miss?" the cab driver asks.

"Can you drive around and show me L.A?" I say, knowing we have to get this car moving or Ty will be right behind us.

"Sure, happy to do that," he says as we pull into the congested Friday night traffic. He begins pointing out areas of interest to me. I don't know how long it's been, maybe a minute or five or maybe hours but I feel his eyes on me in the rearview mirror and hear a heavy sigh.

"Miss, you want me to keep driving? It's been over an hour and the meter's still running. Is there somewhere you need me to drop you?" he says.

"Take me back to Prestian Corp. I've seen enough," I say.

"You got it," he says, navigating through the streets before pulling in front of the chrome and glass sky-rise. I start to swipe my Visa through the slider on the back of the front seat, but then think better of it. Instead, I give him a wad of cash with an overly generous tip and walk into the lobby, taking a quick right before heading up the private elevators. He knows I'm staying here, he'll figure out which room I'm in. I dig the master keycard provided to me for tours out of my purse and stop the elevator on the floor below my own knowing it will be empty for a while.

I drag the dining room chairs in front of the door, piling them with glass dishes. He'll come for me but I'll hear him. My breathing is shallow and I am so cold. I kick off my shoes and slide into the king-size bed, pulling my knees up, tugging the cover over my body right up to my chin. He wants to hurt me again, the same way he did before. I will never be free of him. The feeling of despair and fear continue rolling over me and all my mind can think about is that night. Fighting against the restraints until my wrists were bleeding, the blinding pain, his evil smile as he hurt me over and over.

My entire body jerks with the memory and I swallow a wave of nausea as I wake. "Easy, you're safe Sweetheart," Brian says, pushing the hair out of my eyes and rubbing my back. He's holding me so tight and the beating of his heart is calming to me. Matt is in the corner of the room watching me and gives me a smile. The fogginess in my brain is starting to lift, slowly, as I drift back to sleep.

.

TWELVE

BRIAN

We should be landing at the private strip of the O'Hare airport soon when Matt begins texting on his phone and the descent course changes. "Matt, what's going on?" I ask.

"Jay doesn't want to set us down until he's got control of the airport. Alfreita's men are all over the strip," he says.

"What's the plan?" I say, trying not to wake Jenny as I climb off the couch.

"They've created a diversion. Paparazzi think Alfreita's limos are for some rock star who's about to land. They're not getting past the camera crews very quickly," Matts says.

"Excellent but that's only going to give us a short window of time. When we touch down, have the helicopter take us to my condo. Chase's estate is too far for safety tonight," I say.

"I'll send Jay a note. Your security isn't as good as Prestian's but I agree, it's too far now and too risky. Our crews can keep them busy for a short time," Matt says.

I send Chase a quick text letting the comment about my security go. Little smart ass hasn't even seen my security yet.

Message: Alfreita's men are all over the airport. Her place is not safe-taking her to mine.

Reply: Roger that! Thanks, Brian.

As soon as the pilot gets the go-ahead the descent is quick and he lands it with precision, taxiing us in as close to the awaiting helicopter as possible. I pick Jenny's limp body up and am surrounded by the security team as I carry her across the tarmac to the awaiting chopper. I make a mental note to thank Jay for arranging the fastest of the fleet for our travel. The other limos across the airstrip are encircled by a flood of paparazzi and I smile broadly at the sight and sounds of the approaching police cars. "Let's get this bird in the air," Matt shouts over the blades as we onboard and the door to the cabin closes.

"We've got teams on the rooftop and aerial support is holding two of Alfreita's copters a short distance from the city but let's keep our eyes open. We'll be landing soon," Matt says, relaying a message from Jay.

"Good, keep the snipers on alert. My men just joined your team on the rooftop," I say, reading a message from Scottie.

Matt looks as though he's going to say something but glances at Jenny and decides against it. He's smart to hold his tongue because whether he likes it or not my security team will be there protecting us.

I glance at Jenny. Those deep green eyes are wide and fearful but they're taking everything in. She's alert and knows what's going on. It's the first clear indication that someone's home I've had.

We are heavily escorted as we land. I carry her into the private elevator that opens into my penthouse. It encompasses three floors of the largest sky-rise in the most prestigious area of the city. Home sweet home.

Matt and the security teams follow me into the living room. I attempt to place Jenny on the sofa but she has a death grip around my neck. Her eyes dart warily around the room but soften when she sees Matt. It's clear she trusts him. I sit down on the couch and eventually her grip on my neck eases as the men talk and settle into dining room chairs and bar stools. Celia, my household manager, lays out fresh bread, brie, an assortment of sliced cheese, grapes, and nuts for the men and pretty soon the condo is filled with the fresh aroma of brewed coffee.

"Celia, would you get me a glass of water, please?" I say, realizing it's been some time since Jenny ate or drank anything.

I slide her off my lap, settling her in next to me and I could swear a look of loss or regret flashes in her eyes. I feel it too, Sweetheart. I'd love any excuse to keep her in my arms but the men are looking on and instead I offer her the glass of water.

She takes it out of my hands and I have to hold on to it to keep her from swallowing it all at once. "Easy there, slow at first," I say, capturing a bit that has spilled from the corner of her mouth with the tip of my finger. Her eyes follow the movement. She continues to drink small sips but doesn't stop until I pull the glass away.

"Take a break or you'll be sick," I say, grasping it from her hands. I pick up a piece of the soft torn bread smothered with brie and hold it to her lips. She tentatively takes a bite, looking around. Her face gently flushes and that wonderful little blush appears. She's embarrassed about the fuss. Good, more emotion.

The chiming of the doorbell almost causes her to choke. "Goddamn it," I murmur under my breath as we wait for my security men and Matt's team to clear whoever it is that has arrived unannounced.

"What a team of rowdy looking blokes," Scottie says, walking through the door.

"You're a fucking welcome sight for sore eyes," I say, grasping his hand. "You flew in from London?"

"Jay called and told me someone needed to get you sorted. Is this the wee lass? I can certainly see what all the fuss is about now," he says.

I glare at him. "What's the plan, smart ass?"

He laughs out loud and the men are all pretending to eat or drink to hide their amusement.

"Which of you is Matt?" Scottie says, speaking to the Prestian group.

"That would be me, sir," Matt says, standing up from the seat he's been occupying and extending his hand.

"I go by Scottie, son. Jay tells me you'll be running ops here on the ground from the Prestian side. Two things we need to get clear. First there's a trust issue with your team. The young man who was to guard Jenny failed at the elevator and then again when he left his post outside of her room. Jay tells me you sent him home and recommended his removal from your team."

"Yes, sir. I'll own responsibility for the elevator situation, but he had clear directions not to leave the post outside her door for any reason without getting backup. While it sounds like there may have been some underlying circumstances, bad sushi and all that, he didn't call for help and I can't trust Jenny's well-being to him," Matt says.

"Very good, lad. Jay has great confidence in your abilities and hearing that confirms it for me. As you know, we're dealing with two things; Alfreita and Ty."

I glance at Jenny and at the mention of his name the color drains from her face and the pulse in her neck begins to palpitate. "Scottie, there's a vacant floor in the sky-rise, let's move the briefing to that space. Leave a few men outside the door and we'll be fine until you and Matt return. You can give me an update later," I say and catch the chin nod that Matt sends my way as he leads them out of the apartment.

Celia hands platters of food to the men who look at me. "Take them or she'll send my ass to deliver them to you," I say, shaking my head.

"Thanks, Brian," one says, trying to keep a straight face as they haul the goods out of the room with them.

Celia fusses with setting a smaller plate of cheese and bread in front of us before discreetly disappearing, leaving me completely alone with Jenny for the first time since she kicked me in the balls. I take her hand in mine. She doesn't flinch but instead grasps it tightly.

"No one's going to hurt you while I'm around. I need you to nod if you understand what I'm saying," I say. She nods immediately.

"Can you verbalize that Sweetheart? Say the word 'okay'." There's the emotion again, swirling around on her face.

"Okay," she says finally, licking her lips afterward as though the effort hurt her lips.

"Good girl. You trust me?"

She nods. "Yes."

I stroke her cheek. So fucking soft and creamy. "You've had a rough couple of days. Would you like to take a nap?" I ask.

She blushes. I know she's remembering the last nap she took on the airplane and my cock twitches with the memory. I scoop her up and her arms do not hesitate, immediately locking around my neck but not clutching me like she was before. She's just hanging on while I transport her to the spare bedroom adjacent to my own. It's never been used before and I look around thankful to Celia for always keeping my home on the ready for guests even in the absence of any. I balance her with one hand while I pull back the covers and lay her gently on the bed. Her long dark hair spills out around her and I push it back from her face, taking in her beauty. I pull the covers over her fully dressed body and am about to turn away when she places her hand on mine. "Stay."

I look down at her and my body accepts the invitation before my brain can stop it. I toe off my shoes, pull back the covers, and completely dressed slide in next to her, pulling the covers over both of us.

I send a message to Scottie to let him know not to disturb us for the next couple of hours. She nestles into my arms and lays her head on my chest. I wonder if she can feel the increased beat of my heart as I hold her warm little body close to mine but if she does there's no indication. She nuzzles into my chest, finds my heartbeat and in a matter of moments is sleeping soundly.

I wake painfully aware that my cock has an eager and erect presence. I get up and put my shoes back on making my way quietly to the bathroom to wash up and let my member settle down before heading into the dining room. Scottie is drinking a scotch and looks up from his notebook when I walk in.

"She's still asleep. You have an update?" I say, pouring myself a finger and joining him at the table.

"Jay's got the situation with Alfreita under control, but it's going to be fairly intense the next couple of days. If you don't want to end up involved in the heat between the Larussio mob and Alfreita then we should plan to get Jenny safely to the Prestian Corp towers or his estate as quickly as possible," he says.

"No, she's staying here," I say before my brain can react.

He nods. "That's what I thought you might say, so here's the plan. Matt is settling downstairs and he's already been trained on the safe room and protocols. You'll have two guards outside of this floor, another one on the lower level stairway and the perimeters including rooftops are completely secured."

"What about Ty?" I ask.

"We've got round the clock security on him," he starts, but I cut him off.

"Not good enough Scottie, dig up what you can. I want that fucker behind bars or buried," I say.

"I never thought I'd see a woman get you into a spin. Mr. cool, calm, and collected is a hot-head all of a sudden," he drawls.

"Don't you have work to do instead of harassing my ass? Maybe dig into finding out who Ty worked with at the pharmaceutical companies, who his enemies are?" I counter.

"Already on it, lad," he says, closing his notebook and packing his belongings into the bag lying on the chair next to him. "I'm staying in the security suite, at least until this blows over," he says.

"Good. Thanks, Scottie," I say, opening my notebook as he leaves the condo. I pour myself a cup of coffee and spend the next two hours reviewing Carrington stocks and productivity reports. After Thursday's meeting it was clear that I'll need to make some immediate changes which are bound to be disruptive. I close the Mac an hour or so later and glance up.

She's staring at me from the doorway. "Hi," she says, softly padding into the dining room in bare feet and little French tipped toes. I glance at the kitchen clock. It's ten p.m.

"I thought you might sleep through the night. You haven't

rested in so long," I say, gesturing for her to take a seat at the table.

"I know," she says and I listen in wonder to the melodic tone of her voice. Is there nothing about this woman that doesn't captivate me?

"Would you like something to eat?" I ask, realizing that I'm hungry too and get up to look into the refrigerator. "Shepherd's pie." Celia must have made it knowing that Scottie was coming around. I smile lifting the tin foil to see two pieces have disappeared. He probably scarfed them down while we were sleeping.

"Would you like some?" I ask.

"I haven't had shepherd's pie in years. My mom used to make that. Yes, please," she says, watching me as I put a few pieces on plates and stick them in the microwave before pouring each of us a glass of crisp white wine.

I hand her a plate and she's almost done with her meal before mine is half finished. "That's seriously hungry," I say and her pale face flushes. She puts her fork down and I immediately feel remorse.

"I'm teasing you Jenny. Eat, please, there's plenty in the refrigerator."

She picks up her fork and takes another bite. "It's so good," she says before taking a sip of her wine.

"Couldn't agree more. Celia is a fabulous cook," I say, finishing my own.

"Where is she?" Jenny asks, looking around. I wonder if she's nervous now that it's just the two of us. "The condo has three levels and she has a suite downstairs. Would you feel more comfortable if I asked her to sleep in one of the spare rooms on this floor tonight?"

She contemplates the question before she answers. "No, not really. I was just curious," she says.

"Well just in case you decide I can't be trusted and you want to practice your kick-boxing technique, I've purchased a rather good jock strap," I say.

She actually laughs out loud and turns crimson. "I'm so sorry, I don't know what came over me," she says, looking down.

"Well that's not really true, is it Jenny?" I ask, setting my glass down on the table.

"Maybe not," she concedes, looking up and into my eyes.

"I think you know exactly why you shut down and I won't allow you to diminish how horrible what you must have experienced was by hiding it. It gives the fucker power over you," I say.

She looks taken aback and I wonder if I've pushed too hard, too soon. Shit, it hasn't even been twenty-four hours.

"You know what happened?" she asks.

"Not the details but a pretty good idea," I say.

She contemplates this for a few moments and nods. "You're right. That's why," she says, taking a large gulp of her drink.

"I would sip that wine, because three glasses will be your limit while you're in my care, not three bottles," I say.

"Last time I checked I was of legal age," she snaps.

"Glad to see you've got your sassy mouth and sharp little tongue back," I say, leaning into my chair while taking in her flushed face and deepening color of her narrowed eyes. She is incredibly beautiful when she's angry with me.

"And how do you know so much about me? Have you been stalking me? Should I be afraid?"

"That's not very nice, Jenny. In fact I'm hurt," I say, holding my hand to my heart in jest and to my surprise tears form in her eyes and begin to fall down her cheeks.

"I'm really sorry. I shouldn't have said that. I know you took care of me and got me away from him," she says.

I reach over the table and take her hand and damn if the same electricity isn't there. I rub her hand with my thumb. "It's okay, but I did mean what I said about the alcohol and keeping things bottled up. If you continue down that path you will self-destruct and I'm not going to let that happen."

She looks as surprised at the vehemence in my voice as I feel at my words.

"How do you know so much about me?"

"I tend to want to know a little bit about anyone that tries to kick my balls. Call it self-preservation," I say and she laughs, wiping away her tears.

"So you were stalking?"

"Maybe a bit, but on a serious note, I've been in contact with your counselor. I sent her a note letting her know that you would like to meet with her here. I'll pay her for the trouble," I say.

She looks pissed at first and I prepare for her wrath, but instead she shakes her head and sips her wine. "I know you're only trying to help and I appreciate that, but I don't know what to say to her. It's not that she doesn't know what happened but I didn't tell her all the details." I nod, knowing that if I hear them myself that asshole may not live to see another day. "Can I have another glass of wine?" she asks and I get up to pour her one.

"I can have Kate call you tomorrow. She's been worried sick about you," I say.

"Not yet, I don't feel like I can talk to either of them just yet," she says, sipping her wine.

"Very well," I say, making a note to send Kate an update and reschedule her counselor to the following day. I'll give her one more day but no longer than that.

"Do you mind if I take a shower?" she asks, seemingly embarrassed by the request.

"Of course. You'll find a robe on the door of your bathroom and clothes in the closet and dresser drawers. I had Celia connect with Kate earlier," I say.

"Thank you," she says, taking her wine and heading toward her bedroom. I can't help but watch her body; the long legs in thin yoga pants leave little to the imagination and give me the perfect view of her firm heart-shaped ass and long waist. I drink her in as she walks away taking another sip of her wine. I sign on to check for emails from Scottie, but there's no detailed report on Ty yet.

I hear the blow dryer about a half an hour later and glance up when it stops. She walks across the living room in a long belted robe which emphasizes her tiny waist and all I can do is try to avoid gawking at her chest. She is fucking gorgeous. Her nipples are firm and erect, poking against the thin material and her breasts bounce slightly as she walks toward me. Sweet Jesus!

"Would you like another glass?" she asks sweetly, making her way to the bar and pouring herself a glass of wine.

I smirk. "Sure, a small one, last glass though," I say and she scowls.

"Put your pretty little pout away. Three glasses is plenty for anyone. If you have a difficult time sleeping you can drink some herbal tea that can be paired with alcohol," I say.

She pours one small glass for me and fills her glass to the very top, grinning mischievously at me.

"You know if you didn't just go through such a traumatic experience I'd put you over my knee, lift that robe and spank that pretty little ass of yours for being so sassy," I say, watching her reaction over the top of my glass.

Her face flushes light pink and instead of averting her eyes, she looks into mine and the flash of interest and desire makes my cock twitch. She liked the sound of that. Well so did I, more than she will ever know.

"I think I'll turn in. Maybe read for a while until I can fall asleep," she says.

"Very well, Jenny. Sleep well," I say, watching her walk

back to her bedroom. Damn that body and the throbbing cock she's left me with.

I finish my drink while responding to emails before putting the wine into its refrigerator, locking the door and returning the key to the top drawer of the desk. I open the cupboard, pull out a box of herbal tea and lay it next to the teapot on the stove. Just in case she can't sleep.

I wake a couple hours later to the sound of glass shattering, jump out of bed, and race towards it. I turn on the light and she is in the living room, holding my bottle of scotch in her hands. I gauge just how much she's had by the amount left in the bottom of the bottle and shattered crystal on the floor.

I'm sorry I woke you, I was trying to be quiet," she says, holding a finger to her lips and giggling.

"Well it's a little bit late for that now, isn't it," I say, walking to the closet that holds the cordless vacuum. The mess is minimal and I sweep up the shards that are visible making a mental note to have the room thoroughly cleaned tomorrow.

"So what part of three drinks didn't you understand?" I ask, coming to stand next to her and taking what's left of my bottle of scotch from her hands.

"You said three glasses of wine, you never said anything about scotch," she slurs defiantly.

I narrow my eyes at her. "I would like nothing better than to put you over my knee and watch your ass turn from ivory to red, but gentlemen that I am, I think we'll save that for a time when you're not three sheets to the wind."

"You think I'm drunk," she challenges.

I look at my downed bottle. "Oh, I'm pretty sure that sums it up all right," I say.

"Well, I'm not even a little drunk, not tired, and maybe I'd like to get spanked," she says petulantly.

It's my turn to look at her in surprise. "You're going back to bed where you won't fall and break your neck and since you like to get spanked we'll put it on the calendar for another day," I say, scooping her up.

She wraps her hands around my neck and nuzzles into my chest. "You wouldn't dare," she says before passing out in my arms.

I look down at her as I place her into bed. "I most certainly would Sweetheart," I say, pulling the covers over her, closing the door and returning to my room.

I slide into bed and my cock doesn't want to go down thinking about the gorgeous spirited beauty that's sleeping in the bedroom next to mine but after some time exhaustion finally takes its toll. I am roused a couple hours later by a bloodcurdling scream. It takes me less than a minute to get out of bed and race into her room.

The light from the city is enough to display her body tossing and turning, fighting and struggling under the covers. "Goddamn it," I say aloud, reaching her and gently shaking her awake. "Jenny, you're safe. It's just a bad dream. It's Brian, open your beautiful eyes," I say, stroking her now naked shoulders, trying to dispel the trembling that has overtaken her body as she struggles to come to.

She looks into my eyes as soon as she's awake and squints at me. "Brian," she says, reaching for my hand. We're back to clutching. She's not letting my hand loose anytime soon. "Turn over and I'll rub your back," I say.

She pulls the cover up to her neck all of a sudden realizing that she's naked on top. Definitely not how I left her. "Flip over and let me rub your back," I repeat.

She does and I gently massage the blades between her shoulders and upper back. She moans and my cock throbs against my pajama bottoms, the only barrier that I have. Another twenty minutes and her breathing is even and relaxed. "Good night, Jenny," I say, pulling the comforter up.

She flips over though, keeping a grip on the quilt to remain covered. "Stay, please. Just sleep with me," she says, her eyes wide and pleading.

"Scoot over," I say, maybe a little too gruffly as I slide in next to her. Sweet Jesus, it's going to be torture to sleep next to her all night and not touch her. I lie on my back and pull her face to my chest, knowing that if I curl up with her from behind she'll feel my raging hard on.

Even in her haze, she finds my heartbeat right away and is soon back to sleep. I push the hair out of her eyes and look down at the dark haired angel on my chest and just watch her sleep for what seems like forever before I doze off.

I wake a few hours later to soft moans and legs wrapped

around me, pulling me closer and tighter to her body. "Oh, God Brian, don't stop, please," she whispers hoarsely.

"Fuck me!" She's writhing against my leg and I can feel her heat through my pajama pants and my cock is pulsing like a fucking freight train.

"Wake up, Jenny," I say, shaking her shoulder lightly, not wanting her to feel compromised by an alcohol induced sleep.

"Yes, right there," she moans, shuddering and trembling against my thigh, wrapping her arms around my waist as her climax starts to subside.

Fuck me! My cock is ready for action. "Jenny, wake up," I whisper, shaking her shoulder just a little, trying to wake but not frighten her.

She starts and turns to look up at me. Her legs are still wrapped tightly around mine and I know she can feel the rigidity of my desire lying on my belly. "Oh, God, Brian, I am so sorry," she says, when she realizes that she wasn't dreaming.

I tilt her chin up and wipe the tears that have begun to fall.

"You have nothing to be embarrassed or sorry for. I like the way you feel against me." I take her hand and guide it to my raging hard on. "Feel this?" That's me wanting you in the worst way, but I didn't want to take advantage of you while you're in this state."

Her eyes flash. "You think I'm too messed up in the head or that I'm drunk or hungover?" she says.

"I don't think you're messed up but I do think you've been hurt so bad that it's left an incredible wound and you've only started to heal. That scar got opened back up when Ty got in your face. She blanches at the sound of his name and I immediately feel bad, but she has to face it in order for her to want to get help and eventually heal.

She contemplates this for a long while. She lays her head on my chest finding my heartbeat but doesn't unravel her legs from mine. Then she begins talking, softly, barely a whisper and at first I think I may be imagining it.

"We weren't dating long at all but were practically living together towards the end. I really thought it was the real deal and that one day we would get married."

"What changed?" I prompt.

"Ty leaked information he got from my emails about the Prestian Corp medical expansion plans to the pharmaceutical companies and union heads. He told them changes to the Prestian healthcare package were so severe that it would deplete their future revenues. The pharm companies paid him millions of dollars for more information about the plans. He got the unions all worked up the same way, telling them that Prestian Corp wouldn't be using their workers on any of the new facilities being planned and I know they paid him a lot of money for other information, too."

I make a mental note to have Scottie dig around and find out a little bit more about Mancini's involvement. Nothing happens in the unions without Mancini's involvement.

"After Chase found out what Ty was up to he had to meet with the pharmacy companies and union reps to get it all straightened out. I'm not exactly sure of the details but Chase basically exposed his manipulation and they made him return the money."

If Ty took extorted money from the unions I'm surprised he's still alive and walking. No one crosses Dominic Mancini. She's telling me everything except what happened to her. I can see the indecision swirling in her big green eyes. "You don't have to tell me," I say, running my finger down her cheek.

"Chase set up a meeting with Ty in my office to let him know it was over. On the way home Ty got a phone call and found out he had to pay the money back. He was furious, swerving around cars and driving like a maniac. I should have gotten out of the car, gone back to my place or something, but I didn't. We went back to his house and he started yelling and screaming. He blamed me for Chase finding out and was in an evil mood." She pauses and her breath catches.

"Jenny if this is too much," I start but she keeps talking. "He tied me up and raped me. He was brutal, over and over again until I don't remember quite everything and I guess he finally had enough," she says. She's not crying, she's just very quiet.

"I'm so sorry Sweetheart," I say, pulling her close, trying desperately to keep my anger in check and help her through this without losing my shit. My pulse is pounding and I want nothing more than to snuff the fucking life out of that prick.

"He told me if I ever said a word he would go to the police with evidence that I was using Torzial to launder money and I would go to prison. He was my lawyer, he had all the access he needed and had been laundering money through Torzial for a while," she says.

"Scottie did some research and found out shortly after that Ty's apartment was broken into. You must have told Chase," I say.

"Hmm. You were stalking me?" she says but she doesn't appear mad. "I didn't tell him, but I told Kate. She came over and helped me that night. I made her promise not to say anything but she must have told Chase. Jay had teams ransack Ty's apartment and office that night. They extracted everything out of his computer so he couldn't hold anything over my head in the future."

"That makes sense, but why isn't the fucker in jail?" I ask.

She shrugs. "I couldn't face him in court, didn't want to press charges but then he got attacked. They tied him up and barely left him alive. Tony Larussio's gang was working with Alfreita and wanted to make it look like Carlos Larussio, Kate's dad was guilty."

It all clicks into place for me now. "Yeah, they left the Larussio markings," I say, recalling it from Scottie's report. Maybe Dominic Mancini thought he got what was coming to him, but I still can't imagine him not wanting his own personal pound of flesh.

She nods. "It was pretty gruesome, and I know it's sick, but at the time I somehow felt glad that he got what he deserved," she says.

"There's nothing wrong with that. It's a completely natural

reaction and he hasn't gotten half of what he should have," I say.

"I lied when I said I'm not messed up, because I am. That's why I lashed out that night. I was so turned on but then all of a sudden this feeling came over me."

"What feeling? What happened," I ask, pushing the long strand of curl out of her eyes and behind her ear.

"I couldn't move my wrists and all the fear and panic just got the best of me. I really am sorry," she says.

Her hand is absently rubbing my navel and I have to will myself to breathe regularly. "No need to apologize. I'd like to think I wouldn't have been so forward if I had known but I wanted you in the worst way," I say.

"As in past tense," she says, looking away.

I reach for her hand and place it on my cock again and she moans. Goddamn!

"I haven't been with someone since it happened," she says softly. I do the math, it's only been a few months, but that's a long fucking time without touching anyone or having them touch you.

"I tried by myself, but that didn't work either," she says and her hand is still lying on my cock, every once in a while rubbing.

I struggle with her meaning at first, but then the light comes on. Shit, she hasn't even been able to masturbate.

"Until the night after I met you," she says and I think my cock literally jerks underneath her palm.

"Christmas?"

"Uh-huh. I fell asleep thinking about you and had this deliciously erotic dream and well, it happened in my sleep," she says.

I tilt her face towards me so I can see her eyes. Her thighs tighten around my legs and her hand rubs my cock. Her breathing is shallow, and her cheeks are flushed just like the night I met her. Her lips are quivering and they are so close, I lean down and tilt her chin to mine, holding her eyes captured. Her desire mirrors my own and I take her lips, pleased when she moans against my mouth. She's so responsive. I kiss her, drinking her in, exploring her, our tongues entwining, stoking the passion that has been simmering since I laid eyes on her and is now at a full rolling boil. She moans again and I suckle her bottom lip, pushing her hair out of her eyes. "We're going to use safe words today. If you get to a place where you want to keep going, but you're overwhelmed or struggling emotionally I want you to say yellow, if you want me to stop anything that I'm doing for whatever reason I want you to say red. Understand?" I ask.

She nods. "I need verbal. What's your emotional safe word?" I ask.

"Yellow."

"And if you want me to stop immediately?"

"Red."

"You're sure you're ready?" I ask, suckling the tender flesh of her neck and relishing in the goosebumps I feel appearing on her arms and legs.

"Yes," she says, her legs tightening around my thighs in response to my question.

I roll her back slightly and pull the cover down. Her beautiful breasts are high and firm, the perfect size, not too small, not too large, but fucking perfect. Her nipples are little pink nubs, just begging me to touch them. I stroke one with a single finger, just a light touch and she pushes into me. I roll it between my fingers and thumb applying pressure and feel her legs tighten their grip on my thighs in response. They're connected to the very center of her heat. I suck the nipple captured between my fingers. She moans and my cock twitches and expands. I shift my body, settling in between her legs, trying to keep my weight off her body in case it feels constraining. I kiss her navel and she giggles. She's ticklish, more fun another time. I slide back up and kiss her lips gently, pulling on the bottom one as I break our kiss so I can slide my mouth down the length of her creamy neck.

She moans when I gently squeeze both nipples and my cock delights in her response. Her breath hitches as I slide lower, she knows what I want and her little belly tightens. I let nothing but my breath drift over her arousal and breathe deeply. Her scent is intoxicating and I want to devour her, but instead, I take my time, blowing on the fine hair before letting my tongue wash over her, parting her lips to find the pulsing little nub. I flick my tongue over it and she groans, her hands find their way to my hair and she grasps me closer. I capture it and suckle, she squirms and her hips rise to meet me. Her responsiveness is enough to push me over the edge. Sweet Jesus, she is so wet. She moves her hips again and I take both of her thighs in my hands, pushing them outward, spreading her wider.

I feel her tense, and pause, waiting to see if she needs her safe word, but it doesn't come. I stroke the inside of her thighs and push them outward again, waiting, giving her time to acclimate and then lick and intermittently suckle her clit. I smile when she finally stops pushing against my hands and her legs relax, her hips push up and I reward her by suckling her clit until I can hear her panting and moaning and she begins trembling around me.

"Brian, stop, oh God, it's so good. Stop," she moans. I keep sucking, she knows her safe words. I am greedy for everything she has to give and by the time I'm done she's ridden through two more orgasms. I stroke the length of her thighs with my fingers and her hand is in my hair pulling me closer as I kiss my way up her body, gently nipping each nipple with my teeth. She lets out a little sigh as I settle in next to her and kiss her gently.

She breaks the kiss. "That was amazing, Brian. I want to pleasure you, too," she says shyly and the look she gives me sends my raging cock into overdrive.

I flinch in remorse. I wonder what she'd think if she knew that from the very first time I saw her I wanted to tie her up on my bed, paddle her ass and then fuck her until she begged me to stop and could barely breathe. "Sweetheart, you've already pleasured me more than you know. Sleep for a couple more hours," I say, pulling her close. As soon as she finds my heartbeat, she nuzzles in and drifts off to sleep.

Never in a thousand years would I think that I'd have a girl in my bed and not fuck her, but allow them to sleep with me until morning. I shake my head and instead of getting up to get more work done, I pull her tightly against me and get lost in the feel of her body lying next to mine until my cock finally settles and sleep overtakes me.

I awake to an empty bed and grimace at my pulsing member, which is not likely to go down without a cold shower and a repeat of my hand. I slip out of her bedroom to my own and jump in the shower. In short order I'm pilfering through my closet and instead of a suit grab a pair of jeans and white t-shirt knowing we'll be working from home today.

I head into the kitchen to find Jenny flipping an overstuffed omelet onto a plate. She looks up and her eyes drift down to my cock. Fuck me, she's checking me out and my cock twitches to let her know he's there. I let my eyes linger over her body. Somehow she's managed to steal one of my t-shirts. It barely reaches her thighs and she looks sexy as hell. I focus my gaze on her tits and am rewarded as they become erect before my very eyes.

"Nice outfit," I say, giving her one more glance as I pour myself a cup of the freshly brewed coffee and refill her half empty one.

"Thanks. I didn't expect you to be up this early with as

many times as you were woken up," she says, flushing.

I usually get up around four thirty so this is sleeping in, but I have to admit it's not often that I'm wakened by drunken thieves trying to cart off my favorite scotch while they break my crystal glasses, and then captivate and seduce me in my guest bed," I say.

Her cheeks heat up and my cock expands. The look of embarrassment on her lovely face turns me on. "Well, the first part seems accurate, but I definitely didn't seduce you," she says, looking down and busying herself with breakfast.

I was trying to be a gentleman, not take advantage of her, and she feels remorse that I didn't bang her. She's not looking at me, instead she's looking anywhere but at me and her face is flushed. That's the submissive fucking look I was first drawn to.

"Look at me. You've overcome the ability not to talk, opened up and shared what happened with me, and let me spread your legs and pleasure you which was the most seductive thing you could have done," I say, looking directly into her startled eyes.

She blushes crimson. "It was amazing, you made me feel safe and I will always be grateful for what you did. It's okay if you didn't want the same thing," she says.

She thinks I don't want her and that's why she didn't stay in bed this morning. Shit. I round the breakfast bar and take the plate of omelets and place it into the microwave. "I think breakfast will wait. You've misread the signals," I say, scooping her into my arms and carrying her into my bedroom.

I let her glide down my body in front of the bed so she can feel how hard I am, enjoying the widening of her eyes and the hitch in her breath before her feet touch the ground. "You think I didn't want you? That you were the only one aroused? I thought we had this conversation before," I say, taking the bottom of her t-shirt and beginning to raise it, pausing, making sure one last time this is really what she wants and the soft little moan is answer enough. I pull it above her head and toss it onto the floor. She is standing totally nude in front of me and I'm not quite sure how I want to handle this fragile, delicate little creature.

"You have a magnificent body, Jenny," I say, running my hand down the expanse of her curves, small firm breasts that fit perfectly in the palm of my hand, tiny waist and curvy hips. My lips follow the trail and I revel in her little moans as I kiss the tender skin behind her ear and make my way down her delicate creamy throat. I push her hair out of my way, the soft and silky tendrils running right through my fingers. I kiss her lips again, not sure if I will ever get enough of the way they feel, like honey around my own.

"I think we'll start over," I say, gently pushing her onto the bed, enjoying her look of surprise. I rub her nipples between my forefinger and thumb, applying pressure to the sensitive skin. Her hips move of their own accord and I know her nipples have a direct line to the center of her desire. I squeeze a little harder testing her response and she moans. Fuck she's hot. I nip one of her nipples with my teeth while it's captured between my fingers and she squeals. That's going to be a sound I want to recreate time and time again.

I slowly make my way down her body, caressing the tender skin of the inside of her thighs, teasing her and then trailing my finger around her mound, avoiding its heat. She can only take it so long before she's raising her perfect little ass causing me to give in sooner than I should, letting my tongue trail the sensitive path along her inner thighs, around her mound and then into her wetness.

As soon as my tongue touches her clit, her body tenses, rising up to meet me. I plunge a finger into her hot wet slit before slipping in a second. She engulfs them with her tightness and my cock constricts with the thought of what she'll feel like around it. I caress her with my tongue and the taste and scent of her make my balls tighten and cock throb. I feel her clench around my fingers and curl them slightly. I know as soon as I hit the right spot. She moans and grasps the bed sheets as I suckle her clit hard. Her thighs and ass tighten and I can feel how close she is. "Let go, come for me," I instruct and she fucking obeys, trembling around me. Her eyes are glazed over and sated, but I'm not done with her yet.

I don't allow her to come down from her high before pulling her into a sitting position. This will be the first time since Ty and I don't want to cause her pain. "Tell me what you wanted to do earlier," I instruct.

Her cheeks are already warm and her eyes flash with emotion. She knows what she wants and she takes my hard rigid cock in her hands. They feel like velvet, soft and smooth. She slowly rubs my length and takes notice of the pre-cum. She wipes it from the tip and uses it as moisture as she rubs some more. I almost groan aloud as she works her way down to the root, and then back up, squeezing just right. Oh, this girl can give a hand job. "Tell me what you wanted to do last night. I want to hear it from those sexy little lips of yours," I say.

Yes, she likes it when I take charge. It gives her permission to do what she wouldn't ordinarily do. It makes my cock twitch hard in her hand; she feels it and rubs him.

"I wanted to feel my lips wrapped around you, and then I wanted to feel you inside of me. Fucking me," she says after a brief pause.

"Nothing stopping you now, Sweetheart," I say, looking down at her. She does not hesitate, licking my shaft, coating me with her moisture before sliding her smooth, moist lips around my member. She is on her knees kneeling over my cock and all I can see is her soft, beautiful hair spilling around her shoulders and breasts and her lovely little ass gently bobbing in the air while her mouth is around my cock. She takes me deeper and I contain a groan of pleasure, grasping her hair and head to pull her down harder until I need to pull out and cool off before I end up coming in her mouth. "Slow, Sweetheart, we have all day," I say, kissing her lips, tasting myself on her tongue.

"Take my cock and show him where you want him," I instruct.

"Inside of me," she says hesitantly.

"Show me," I say, ripping open the foil pack and slipping the condom in place. That's all I'll do for her. If she wants this she's going to drive. She smiles, grabbing me around the waist and pulling me on top of her as she positions her body and guides my eager cock to the entrance of her mound. She wants me on top, wants me to take charge. Okay, Sweetheart, you had your chance.

I rub my cock at the entrance. It's been a long time since I've been in a missionary position but the raging hard-on I have is eager as fuck to feel her around me, position be damned.

"Ready?" I ask.

"Yes," she says without hesitation, lifting her hips, pressing the heat of her hot little pussy right next to me.

I need no further invitation but restrain myself from pushing into her with one stroke. Instead, I rub myself against her, moistening myself in her juices, teasing her as I push and pull out, then do it again, little by little. When she's adequately stretched and I know I won't hurt her, I push in all the way and she raises her hips to allow me better access.

"Oh, Sweetheart those legs are going to be over my shoulder in a few minutes," I say, holding back the need to bury myself and intensely pound until she comes all over me.

I push into her time and time again, delighting in the emotions on her face. "Have you ever come from penetrative sex?" I ask.

The blush again and she contemplates my question as I dip

in and out. I take her chin and tilt it so she is facing me. "The truth."

"No, but I've faked it a few times," she says after a short while.

"You won't be faking it with me but you're going to need to remember your safe words and let me know if it gets to be too much," I say, pushing farther into her velvety softness, allowing her to build until I feel her tighten around me.

"I'm going to lift your legs. You'll feel me deeper and then I'm going to drive into you fast, over and over until you come all over my balls. If you want me to stop, say so now."

"Green," she says, her eyes darkening with anticipation.

I push her knees to her chest, thrusting forward, the position allowing me to sink into her, balls deep. "Oh, God," she moans.

The look on her face and that little moan let me know that I've hit her g spot, that special little place that is my bullseye from here on home. I slide her legs above my shoulders and as soon as I sink back in she lets out a deep moan, her breath coming fast and furious. She closes her eyes.

"Open your eyes and look at me when you come," I instruct, driving deeper and faster as her walls clench around me and her thighs begin to shake around my neck.

She begins crumbling and I do not let up. "Oh, God Brian, I'm coming," she cries and I keep thrusting, pumping and pumping until I bring us both to release and she is left trembling in the aftermath. Her greedy pussy continues to milk me for all I'm worth causing me to empty everything that I have.

"That was so good," she says, reaching up to kiss my lips. I reposition her, reluctantly letting her legs down and pulling out, slipping out of the condom and tying it off before tucking her into my arms while she finds that spot on my chest that she loves to burrow into.

Her breath is still ragged from exertion and I push the hair from her face, bending down to kiss her forehead. Her breathing pattern changes and I look down in amazement as I realize she is already fast asleep again. This is the time where I usually tell a woman it's been fun, I'll call you and get rid of them as fast as I can and never do. An hour later I wake and she's still resting peacefully. I get out of bed careful not to disturb her as I head into the bathroom for a shower.

I walk back into the bedroom with a towel wrapped around me and pull on my jeans and t-shirt. She's still sleeping soundly, her arm curled around my pillow and her bare back exposed down to the beautiful little curve of her ass. I pull the covers over her gently, trying not to wake her before heading to the kitchen. My stomach growls and I decide to cook something since hours old omelets don't appeal. I feel a pang of guilt, recalling how hungry she was yesterday and how quickly she devoured the shepherd's pie. I open the refrigerator to check our options and turn at the sound of footsteps behind me. "I see you've made a grand mess of my kitchen," Celia says, taking in the omelet pan and left over plates on the stove.

"Jenny will be up soon. We didn't have breakfast and she'll

be hungry," I say, trying to avoid her thinly veiled smile as I take the plate of omelets out of the microwave.

"Poor thing must be starving," she says, pulling one ingredient after another from the refrigerator.

"Cold snowy January day calls for comfort food. How about chicken, rice, and cilantro soup with a fresh salad and homemade buns?" she says.

"Perfect." I pop a K-Cup into the machine and scan the email on my phone for a note from Scottie while I wait, taking my coffee with me into the living room when it's done. Damn it what's taking the guy so long? I send a text.

Message: In-depth report on Ty?

Reply: Soon, almost done.

My phone vibrates and I accept Scottie's call. "We've tracked down the official reports on three of the women that he assaulted. It seems he was able to blackmail his way out of charges. Two were married and one was a professor at his school. Appears he had pictures of all of them they didn't want public. The thing is none of these women were raped, or violated sexually. He lost his temper and beat them up," Scottie says.

The only one he raped was Jenny. I let that settle in for a moment and the knowledge leaves me seething with rage. "I've crossed referenced our information with that of Jay's intel," he says.

I grimace. "Shit, now Chase will want to know why I'm looking into the details," I say.

"I already cleared it through Jay. Told him I wanted the inside scoop on the pretext that Jenny's staying at your home. He and Chase both know we need to know what to be prepared for and with their intel they would have known the minute we started snooping around," he says smoothly.

"This is why you will always work for Carrington Steel as long as I have anything to say about it. Thanks, Scottie," I say.

"The Larussios are working to put Alfreita out of business for good. The way I understand the situation, it's all-out war, but it's almost over," he says.

I'm more concerned with Ty at the moment. "Why the fuck would Chase just let him walk?" I say, fuming.

"I know," Jenny says, walking into the room. Her footsteps were so quiet I didn't hear her approach.

"Call me back when you know more, Scottie," I say, disconnecting and swiveling in my chair to watch her walk toward me. She's dressed in black dress pants that hug the curves of her hips with black fuck me heels and a little sweater that molds to her perfectly formed breasts.

She walks past the couch towards the kitchen counter and says good morning to Celia.

"Favorite flavor," I ask, gesturing to the assortment of coffee flavors. She fingers through the selection of K-Cups on the counter and places one in the machine before pressing the brew button.

"Caramel girl, huh?" I say, thinking to myself that we could have a lot of fun with that another time.

"Uh-huh. Anything caramel," she says, licking her bottom lip.

My dick twitches and I know I'm going to need to adjust at some point. All I can imagine right now is drizzling warm caramel all over my dick and letting her suck it off with those pouty little lips of hers.

She walks into the living room while Celia cooks, her coffee in hand and with an air of confidence I haven't seen since the night of the wedding. I find her intriguing and watch as she settles into the couch, crossing her legs while nestling the cup of coffee in her hand and inhaling the steamy aroma.

"Kate told me Chase had a plan to uncover some of the dealings that Ty had with the pharmaceutical companies. He was pretty close to having him exposed, and then Kate's uncle, the one that was working with Alfreita to gain control of the Larussio market, had him beat him up. His plan to frame Carlos Larussio with the incident didn't work, but it put a halt to what Chase was planning. It would have raised too many questions while Prestian Medical Facilities was trying to negotiate medicinal costs as part of the care service," she says.

I contemplate what she's saying. I had already drawn a similar conclusion about why both Chase and Mancini backed off, but I'm still pissed that the fucker's still walking around. I also know Chase better than anyone. He doesn't let things like this go and neither do the Larussios or Mancini. I don't know what shit storm is about to explode, but we are definitely right in the eye of the twister.

"If you're hungry lunch is ready," Celia says, coming round the dark grey quartz breakfast bar that wraps around the open concept kitchen.

"I'm absolutely ravenous," Jenny says, as I extend my hand to help her from the sofa she's nestled in. She takes it gingerly and smiles at me and something in my throat catches.

What the fuck is wrong with me. This girl is troubled with a capital T and I've let her sleep with me, eat with me, and am seriously contemplating how to keep her safe and protected from not only Ty but all the ugliness in the world. "Come on, I'm hungry, too," I say, guiding her to the smaller of the dining room tables in the corner of the kitchen that overlooks Lake Michigan.

Celia has everything laid out for us and I marvel at how I would get along without her. Jenny is definitely not a salad girl first. She tears a piece of the freshly baked roll and dips it into the aromatic chicken and rice soup, lifting it to her lips before she begins to chew. That face, the movement of her tongue over her lips, pure ecstasy and it makes my dick hard again.

"Anything else you need? If not, I'm going to head over to my office and get our order put in for next week," Celia says, finishing up in the kitchen.

"No, we're good, but could you add a few items to the list?" I ask.

"Of course," she says, sliding me a long magnetic notepad and pen. I hastily write down an order for flowers, a few bottles of my favorite wine which Jenny also seemed to enjoy last evening, and another bottle of my favorite scotch. She glances at the list and then over at the bar where I usually keep it. Not seeing it, she smiles, knowing I would never consume that much alcohol on my own.

I smirk and give her a wink. "So she goes grocery shopping for you?" Jenny says, once Celia's out of earshot.

"Yes, she oversees the penthouse and the staff that take care of it," I say.

She scrunches her lips. "You have more than one person?"

I'm not sure where we're going with this. "Yes, Celia oversees the three part-time people that clean and a fourth that she's taken under her wing in the kitchen."

"Matt sent me a text to let me know he's downstairs and with any intrusion he'll be alerted. What happens if someone breaks in?" she asks.

"One, if anyone is even close to our floors on this building security would have us moved to the safe room. Matt is working with the man Scottie's placed in charge of perimeter security right now and has already been trained in the procedures," I say.

"Okay, and he'll be able to get here fast," she says, looking around the vast suite.

"Would it make you more comfortable to go over the protocols?" I ask, sensing her anxiety with all the strange people in charge of her life. She trusts Matt which is why I made him co-point with my crew. Nothing gets approved without his knowledge and he's part of every huddle.

"I feel completely safe with you, but I don't know your men

and Matt's never been this far away from me. He's been sleeping on my couch since the accident. I guess, well it's just different," she says, finishing her lunch.

I know he's been staying with her since the attack. I try to suppress the green-eyed monster and instead be grateful that Chase has someone protecting her. This woman is clearly very confident and used to having control in her everyday life even if she likes to relinquish it in the bedroom. She trusts him. I send him a text.

Message: Can you come upstairs?

Reply: On my way.

"Matt will be up shortly and go over things with you," I say.

The elevator dings letting me know that Matt has arrived before he walks in. "Thanks for taking the time to stop up. She's a little nervous, new space, people she doesn't know very well," I say.

"No problem, Brian. The crew ran through the drills with me yesterday and we can go over them together," he says, taking a seat at the table.

"Hey, I missed you. I hear they've had you stashed somewhere close by though," she says.

"I'm just a few moments away if I take the private entrance. Jay asked me to be co-point with the Carrington guys so I've been monitoring everything from downstairs," he says.

She glances at me and I can't help but grin. "Monitoring the perimeter and any possible security breaches," I say, bemused at where her runaway thoughts were going.

"Oh, got it," she says, the pink on her cheeks starting to recede.

"I want to go through four scenarios. Even in imminent danger the brain is able to pull on learned memory and recalled physical movement," Matt says.

"I have no issue with that. Let me know what you want Jenny and me to do," I say, having heard the very same thing from Scottie years ago. I don't know where they learn this shit, but I'm glad they do what they do.

"Holy fuck," she says under her breath after he finishes going over the protocols. My family's wealth has always required such security extremes, but to her it is new. I can only hope she believes it's in her best interest as I watch the myriad of emotions cross her features. She is quiet and contemplative while Matt and I talk about the next couple days before he leaves.

"Tell me what's troubling you," I say, when it's just the two of us.

"I don't even know where to start. How long will I be here?" she asks.

"You know the situation with the Larussios and Prestians. It's not safe for you to be on your own or travel to their estate until Alfreita is out of the picture. I don't think it will be too long, but I'll know more after a call with Chase later in the day," I say.

I can tell the reality of the imminent danger has been a lot for her to take in. She just needs someone to take the reins for a while. "I contacted your counselor. She'll be here in a couple hours," I say.

Her brow scrunches with worry as she contemplates this. "Brian, I don't know what I'm going to say and I thought she was coming tomorrow," she says finally.

"She would have but was booked solid for the entire week. You don't have to tell her everything, just what you can talk about for now, but you need to start letting it out, finding a way to heal," I say.

"I didn't realize I was dealing with an expert in psychology Mr. Brian Carrington. Since when did you get doctorate credentials behind your name? While I appreciate your help in getting me out of there and keeping me safe, I think I am the expert on when and who I discuss this with," she says, her glare sharp enough to make most men back down.

Okay, definitely not submissive in nature outside of the bedroom. God she's hot when she lights up! I try to hide my amusement, not recalling a time in years when a woman has chewed me out like this. Most are so interested in pleasing me for a chance at the Carrington pocketbook they would never think to disagree with me.

"What the hell is so funny?" she asks, still glaring at me.

In three long quick strides I reach her, pulling her stiff body towards me, capturing her lips with mine. She opens to me and I don't hesitate, exploring the sweetness within. When I pull away and look down at her the anger in her eyes has calmed slightly, but the storm is still swirling as she watches me.

"I only want what's best for you. You need to talk to someone professionally. She's the best in the industry which is why Chase hired her. Let her come over, see where it goes," I say, kissing her lips again, gently this time, coaxing.

To my surprise tears form in those lovely green eyes and they spill onto her fair porcelain complexion. "Okay, I know I should... it's just I have no idea what to say to her. Why didn't I know he was like this and why couldn't I get him off of me?" she says, crying against my heart.

I pick her up and take her to the couch, keeping her on my lap as she burrows her face in my chest and continues to sob. I pull the afghan from the back of the sofa and place it around her. All I want to do is protect this girl and my raging heart sees red when I think of the son of a bitch that caused this. I rub her back and I don't know how long I sit with her like this until her breathing begins to change, and I look down in wonder at the sleeping form burrowed into my chest. I finally tear myself away and settle her into the couch, covering her before taking a seat at the dining room table to work. A half hour later Scottie's number appears on my cell and I step outside on the balcony to take it so as not to disturb her rest.

"Scottie, what'd you find?"

"Brian, this guy has a bad fucking temper, we're uncovering more all the time. He should have been behind bars long before now, but there is absolutely no history of anything sexual, just an asshole with a violent temper."

I am watching her from the balcony. She awakens, looks

around and spots her phone on the edge of the sofa. She reaches over and picks it up, smiling widely, and begins talking.

"Why her Scottie?"

"Lad, you know I like her son, but is there any chance that she got knocked around and not raped?"

I grit my teeth and control the urge to reach through the phone and throttle him. "No," I grind out.

"Okay son, calm down. It's my job to give you the facts and get to the bottom of things. I'm not sure what's going on between the two of you, but my job is to keep you safe," he says.

"What the hell are you suggesting?" I say.

"I'm merely pointing out the fact that you know very little about this young lady. The only person she told of the incident was Kate who is her best friend, and there was never a police report. Jay had Chase give our teams permission to review the security reports from the two nights leading up to her attack until two days later. She called Kate that night; security took Kate to her house. Kate called Chase a couple hours after she got there and...."

"I've got all this, it's in your bulleted fucking report," I say, grinding my teeth with impatience.

"Lad, what you don't know is that when Matt got there Jenny had been drinking quite a bit. It's documented that Kate told Chase she had never seen Jenny drink so much in her life, and that she tucked her in on the couch when Jenny passed out before she called him. Chase sent Matt and a few men to guard the house and he's been with her ever since. They were supposed to stay on the perimeter, per Chase's orders, but you know Jay. He wanted to find out a little bit more and sent Matt into the house. He took pictures of Jenny's arms. The skin was ripped and bleeding from pulling at her restraints. I have no doubt that whatever the fucker did was painful and she was desperately trying to get out of the situation."

"Then what the hell is the problem, Scottie? What are you questioning?"

"Matt didn't take any genital pics. I would have insisted our crew take them to be sure, or to use later," he says.

"Jesus H, Scottie. What the hell are you getting at?"

"What I'm asking you is if it's at all possible that he didn't rape her?"

"No, Goddamn it, it is not. I know you've got our best teams working day and night with Larussio and Prestian, but bring in more men if you need to. I want to know what means the most to this man, what makes him tick, what his passion is, and once you find it, I am going to fucking destroy him," I say.

"Lad, I will do that. But, make no mistake. I am also going to be digging into why he was able to hold this threat of silence over her. Whether you want to believe it or not, all of the women previous to him had something he could leverage. The patterns aren't matching up son," he says before disconnecting.

I look out over the city and Chicago River below watching the water taxis in the distance make their way up and down carrying tourists and others even in the cold of the winter. I didn't tell him that I know what Ty was holding over her head. That Chase made sure the evidence of money laundering through the Torzial accounts was cleaned up, but she just couldn't bring herself to face him in court.

I glance at Jenny and she is nodding her head as I walk through the sliding glass doors back into the condo.

"I promise, I'll take your advice. Okay, stop worrying. I'll call you once I've talked with her then," she says, pulling the cover over her as the windy Chicago breeze follows me in from the balcony.

"Kate?" I ask, settling in next to her as she disconnects.

"Yeah, her daily call whether I need it or want it," she says, wryly.

"She cares about you. Chase could barely get her out of L.A. when you were missing and she wouldn't give Matt or Jay a moment of peace until we found you," I say.

"She's the best friend I've ever had and I know that must have been hard for her. I feel horrible that she had to let my mom know I was missing and prepare her for the police."

"What do you mean prepare her?"

"I never told my mom about the attack and Kate didn't know that," she says, looking down at her fingernails.

"Why didn't you tell her?"

She shrugs and focuses in on a hangnail. "I couldn't at first and then after it had been a while I decided that telling her in person was probably better. Once I got there I just couldn't ruin her holiday with all this shit. She's been taking care of my brother's kids for a while. You can't know how hard it's been on her since my father died and my brother got in the accident. For the first time in a long time, my mom was really happy and I just couldn't tell her. "

"She's been taking care of your niece and nephew?" I say, pushing the long brunette tendril out of her eyes and behind her ear.

"Yes, raising them and loving them because their parents can't. Their mother struggles with addiction and hasn't been part of their lives for a long time and my brother was in a terrible motorcycle accident. He was always one to live life on the edge, just the opposite of me. My dad and I were a lot alike and very close and he knew I dreamed of starting my own business. When he passed away he left a chunk of his inheritance to me. My father's will said he saw the same passion in me that he had and wanted to give me enough to start a business and take care of our family into the future. I'm trying to do that, Brian. I invested every penny and my dream is starting to come true. Every month I'm able to send more money to my family and put more into our stocks for the future. I have to admit that Torzial couldn't have gotten as far as it is without Chase, though," she says.

I don't tell her that I've read an in-depth report on her or that I know how well she's done for herself. "How'd that come about?" I ask, recalling the portfolio of her investments and Prestian's.

"My company was doing pretty well in Chicago, it was

slowly growing. We got a contract with a health care company in Houston and Kate was the consultant assigned to the project. The quality metrics started coming in and they were impressive. Chase contacted me about a medical center he was subsidizing in the Chicago area. I asked Kate to take it on since she was finished with the Houston case and you can probably guess the rest," she says.

"Yeah, I know how they met. She was working through me for a while before the event. Chase ended up attending with me and they were inseparable after that. She's really passionate about the patient experience."

"Yes, the work is critical, it's changing healthcare dynamics and Chase has a great vision for Prestian Corp Medical. He wants to shake up the industry and get consumers rallied around the fact that they can control their own healthcare, increase quality, and drive down costs at the same time," she says, her eyes alight with the same passion I've seen when Kate talks about the project.

"That's why Ty was able to create a sense of urgency around what Chase was working on. I still can't believe I trusted that bastard. He just saw me as a way to launder his filthy money," she says.

"How long was it going on?"

"I don't even know. I trusted him and he had been my attorney long before we started dating for Christ's sake. I wouldn't have even known if he hadn't told me that if I went to the cops all of my money laundering would be revealed. I didn't have a fucking clue what he was talking about until Chase looked into it."

I am barely able to control my desire to pummel this bastard again, but I can't deny that Scottie has planted a nagging doubt in my mind. "When did you tell anyone about this?"

"I only told Kate, at least most of what happened. She kept encouraging me to go to the hospital."

"That was good advice. Did you go?"

"You think that was good advice? What the hell were the cops supposed to do? It's not like I could press charges against the bastard with everything he threatened me with. I have a family that depends on the money sent to them every month. The promise made to my dad to take care of our family means everything to me," she says, eyes lit up with fury.

"Jenny, I get that, but afterward, after Chase's team removed all doubt why didn't you go after him?" I ask.

I hate the tears in her eyes and the fact that I've caused them, but I need to know. It's burning me up now that Scottie has brought it to the forefront.

She looks at me for a long time and I will myself silent. "I lied when I said I'm not messed up. I am very messed up." The tears in her eyes brim over and I steady myself knowing there are going to be more days like this ahead. "Why are you crying, Jenny?"

"If I dreamt about being held down and it made me come then I must have liked it, just like he said," she says.

Shit, this is so much more than I'm prepared for. "What that fucker did was abuse and you have nothing to be sorry or remorseful for. You are submissive in the bedroom, meaning turned on by the control that someone provides during the coupling. There's nothing to be ashamed of. In fact it turns me on so much that all I want to do is cart you back to my bedroom and have my evil way with you again."

She hides her face in my chest and I allow it for a few moments and then lift her chin. "Tell me what's going on in that pretty little mind of yours," I say.

"You really want to know why I didn't go to court?" she says.

I nod. "At first it was just like I told you. He threatened me with money laundering charges and I really didn't want to face him, but it was more, too." She pauses as if deciding whether she should go on.

"Tell me, I want to hear it," I urge.

"I've never engaged in restrained sex, but I've always thought about what it would be like. I've even researched, read stories, and watched videos."

"I like that very much, keep talking Sweetheart," I say, watching her pupils dilate.

"The images of women being taken while they're in handcuffs, tied with ropes, scarves or whatever, Brian, it really turns me on. Even that night, I knew if I went to the hospital pictures of the tears on my arms would be taken and it would have to be a central point of the discussion in court."

"What makes you think legal council would take that angle?"

"One night I told Ty about my fantasies, showed him one of the sites I was looking at. He didn't say much, but he didn't have to. I saw the look of disgust in his eyes," she says, lowering her eyes.

I raise her chin up. "You don't look down like you're embarrassed by your desires. You weren't asking to be raped; you were sharing your desire for him to take the reins and allow you to explore your needs with him in control. It's the biggest fucking honor and gift any man can receive from his partner," I say.

She contemplates this, chewing her lip and nods. "He's a lawyer for Christ sakes. I was scared his high powered friends would just turn the defense into a guy trying to satisfy his deviant girlfriend and I couldn't risk losing Torzial's reputation. It's my family's bread and butter. Maybe in some sick fucked up part of my brain I thought because I had dreamed of being restrained when I had sex that it wasn't rape and I had caused it," she says.

"Listen to me. The dreams you have are normal. Everyone has different fantasies, different kinks that turn them on. Some people act on them and others don't, but both parties have to trust each other and consent to a relationship or coupling like that. There was no fucking consent there, Jenny. What he did was commit rape, plain and simple and I won't have you blaming yourself. Do you understand?"

She nods, but she's just looking at me taking it all in. "It's done, nothing can take it back, but you need to get out of the way of your own desires. Just because you want a man to take charge in the bedroom doesn't make you weak, actually it's the submissive in the bedroom that has all the power. You come across so self-assured in email and correspondence. Smart, articulate and so fucking confident in the professional world, that and your demureness is what attracted me to you. Your eyes were cast down when I flirted with you. I could feel your breathing change, your skin warm in a blush and when I was dancing with you I could feel your nipples harden. Damn, you're all I could think about for days."

I take her in my arms. "Jenny, our sexual fantasies are just that. What he did to you was abuse and rape and I know you'll never be able to fully get it out of your mind but I'd like to try to make you see how other men behave. Tell me what you liked last night and then tell me what you desire. Your deepest darkest desires," I say, kissing and licking her neck.

She's back to contemplating, but it doesn't take her long. "I think about being spanked, about being restrained, about, well a lot of things, but not hurt like that," she says.

"No one is ever going to abuse you again as long as I'm breathing. I want to teach you and let you experience everything you've dreamed about," I say.

"I'd like that," she says.

"When I slid your hands up the wall the night of the

wedding, you were right to feel the effects of restraint. I wanted you to feel captured and controlled, allowing me to pleasure you. If we had gone further that night, I would have pulled down your panties, put you across my knee and spanked your perfect little ass until it heated to a bright red for turning me on so much. Then when I was through, I would have turned you over and licked your pussy until you came all over my face, and then I would have fucked you, hard, very hard, bent over the desk in that office until you were screaming my name and coming again. But a relationship like that takes trust and that's something that's been taken from you," I say, kissing her lips softly.

"Holy shit. My panties are soaked just listening to you talk. At least now I know what I can talk to the counselor about," she says, taking me completely by fucking surprise.

"I was just wondering how far your submissive tendencies run, but it's clear they don't run very far outside of the bedroom," I say, sardonically.

"Really? What in the world would give you that idea?" she says, trying without success to hide her smile.

"Your ability to tell me exactly what you like and what you don't and your sassiness for starters," I say, smirking at her. I dare her to challenge me on this.

"So do you like your women completely submissive in the bedroom as well as outside of it?" she says.

It's been a long time since I wasn't sure how to answer a question. I decide to be honest. "I love your submissiveness in the bedroom and your sassiness outside of it. I'd like to punish you for some of your behavior though," I say.

"That makes me so wet," she says and I follow her downcast eyes, lifting her chin so she is forced to look at me.

Fuck me. She couldn't be more submissive if she tried. That's all I need. "It would seem we have some punishment for your behavior the last few days that we need to get through before we can move on," I say.

"I'd like to hear about that," she says, her eyes downcast again.

"A spanking for attempting to kick me in the balls, stealing my favorite bottle of scotch, breaking my glass, for making me wake up alone this morning, and another for not telling me you were submissive."

She looks up and holy shit, her deep green eyes seem to have come alive right in front of me. "Five spankings? I believe four are in order. I can't be held responsible for not telling you I was submissive. I didn't know," she says.

Fuck me. She's agreeing to spankings for behavior but doesn't have a clue about her needs as a submissive. My cock twitches in delight but I know I need to go slow.

"How many relationships have you had, Jenny?" I ask.

"A few boyfriends that ended in foreplay, a couple with sex, and then him," she says.

"What kind of sex have you had?" I ask, watching the shades of color on her cheeks turn a warm pink. My dick twitches and my balls contract.

"You mean like what positions?" she asks.

"Sure we can start there," I say, trying hard to hide my bemusement.

She considers my question, chewing her lip. "Well, a few times I was on the bottom and one time in a car. "Oh wait," she says, her eyes lighting up with mischievousness. "And one time I was on the bottom and then got flipped to the top," she says.

"Well I didn't know I was dealing with someone so worldly," I tease, wondering how the hell someone as attractive as her can escape the clutches of a million guys that must have wanted that body and would treat it right.

"Are those your only sexual experiences?" I ask, still baffled.

"No." It comes out stilted, making me glance down into her eyes. They are narrowed and calculating. She's not sure how to talk about the rape.

"You don't have to tell me, Jenny," I say, knowing this may take the skills of her counselor but she ignores me and forges on.

"Ty," she says and it's like she has to spit the word out of her mouth.

"You want to talk about what he did to you?" I ask.

She shivers and I lean down and kiss her, sucking on her bottom lip. "Sweetheart, you can tell the counselor later, or you can feel free to tell me anything," I say.

She chews her lip where I've just been, contemplating. I see only the briefest swirl of indecision in her eyes. "He tied me up with really course rope and slapped me so hard that my lip was split open for a week. Then he put duct tape over my mouth so no one could hear me scream and raped me. He wanted to hurt me, Brian. He was laughing. He raped me repeatedly both vaginally and anally and the pain was intense. When he was done with me he made me suck his cock. It was sickening and I almost choked on my vomit. Then he got tired of me and started using other things. I'm not sure what they were but they were large. They hurt so bad that I finally lost consciousness. When I woke up he was slapping me, laughing at me."

I am reeling with the desire to kill this mother fucker with my own two hands but I will myself to remain calm for her sake. "You never told anyone?"

She shakes her head. "Kate knows I was raped. I didn't plan to tell her but she saw the rope marks on my wrists. I couldn't talk about it at the time. In all honesty, this is the first time I've shared it with anyone."

"Ty is an abusive asshole, Jenny. What he did to you was rape and physical assault. He should be behind bars or dead for what he's done. That has absolutely nothing to do with the fantasies and desires that you've thought about," I say.

She nods, considering what I've said. "Now tell me what you dream about doing in the bedroom," I say.

Her blush is crimson and I realize that she's never acted on anything that turns her on and the cruelty from Ty has gotten in the way of her separating her own desires in the bedroom from abuse. "I won't ask you again, unless you want to add another paddling to your already long list," I say.

This time she doesn't look down. "I had a dream."

"Tell me what happened. I want to hear what turns you on, Sweetheart," I say.

"You had me lay face up on the bed and restrained me with the sapphire tie you were wearing on Christmas Eve. It was long; you tied it around my wrist and a loop in the headboard."

"What did I do to you when you were bound?" I ask, wanting her to lead this part of the conversation.

"You spread my legs like you did last night. Made me feel vulnerable and then you spanked me," she says.

"Sweetheart, you were facing me, where was I spanking you?"

She looks down and her face reddens with embarrassment. It's hotter than hell and my cock twitches inside of my pants.

"Sweet Jesus, was I spanking your pussy while I had you restrained?" I ask.

She doesn't say a word, but nods. My balls contract filled with the need for release but I hold it back. She's opened up to me but she's embarrassed by it. "That's the hottest thing that anyone has ever said to me but you act like you're ashamed that you dreamt it," I say, watching the myriad of emotions spill past her eyes.

"It's hard to reconcile my dreams and what happened in reality," she says almost whispering.

I totally get that. It's on me to go slow. "So let's start with this. What are your safe words?" I ask.

"Yellow, red, and green," she says.

"Green?" I ask, more than a little intrigued.

"Keep going. I read it once," she says, blushing.

I try to hide my amusement at her innocence. "I like that you've read about things like that. I wondered when you said that yesterday." I glance at my phone, scowling as I note the time.

"What's the matter?" she asks.

"As much as I would love to restrain and spank your sweet little pussy, your counselor will be here in less than half an hour and I want much more time with you than that. Why don't you get ready to talk with her and we'll finish this later."

"Okay," she says, smiling up at me as the little blush that sets my dick on fire emerges. I pull her to me, rougher than intended, capturing her lips with my own, groaning as she opens for me and I hear her soft little moans. This woman takes my fucking breath away. I finally break the kiss. "Remember what I said. You have absolutely nothing to be ashamed of, do you understand me? The fact that you would like to be restrained and spanked makes me harder than hell, but I would never, ever, do anything you didn't want or like. It's you who has all the power, you say when, and how you want it. There's a definite difference between enjoying consensual sex and what he did to you. I just wish I had time to show you before you talk to the good doctor," I say, brushing her lips lightly with my own.

She opens up to me and blushes. "Thank you, Brian," she says, kissing my lips gently before she leaves to get ready. I pour myself a glass of ice water from the refrigerator and try to cool down before heading to the study, settling in at my desk for the afternoon. I send Matt a text.

Message: Dr. Werther will be arriving by limo in 20 minutes. She'll be disguised. Please make sure all security precautions are in place and then show her up. Could you stay in the suite until the visit is over?

Reply: Yes, sir.

Message: Matt, the name's Brian. Thanks for your help.

Reply: Thanks, Brian.

THIRTEEN
JENNY

I look down at my clothes and smooth my hair once more before heading out to the living room to greet the counselor. Matt is in the living room with Dr. Werther and I don't see Brian.

"Thank you for coming," I say, extending my hand in welcome. Matt must feel comfortable with her or I know he wouldn't allow her in the suite.

"Would it be okay for us to spend a little time alone together?" I ask him.

"Yes, but I'll be in the room next door and we have men positioned in the hallway and around the perimeter. You'll be perfectly safe," he says, giving Dr. Werther a nod before heading towards the dining room and kitchen beyond.

"I don't think I've ever been in a situation quite like this before," the counselor says, taking off her hat and letting her hair fall around her shoulders.

"Yes, I'm sorry about Matt and all the security. The paparazzi would find out who you were if they didn't disguise you," I say.

"He seems quite protective over you," she says as I lead her into the library.

"He's been with me since the night of the attack," I say, quietly.

She nods, just taking it in. "And then there's the young man that called me. I don't think I had a chance in hell of turning down his request to visit you. He had everything arranged before he contacted me," she says, settling into one of the chairs in the room.

"Yeah, that would be Brian. Welcome to my world," I say, grinning. She is easy to talk to and I find myself relaxing. I have no idea why suddenly after all this time it's no longer as difficult to talk about, but after opening up to Brian and my feelings about the guilt it's easy to share it all with her and I do, right down to every sordid little detail. After two hours, it feels like the weight of the world has been lifted. I agree to meet her on a routine basis for a while and thank her for the repeated attempts at reaching out to me when I didn't show up for appointments before she leaves.

I am contemplating all that I've shared with her and Brian throughout the course of the day when he comes out of his study.

"How did things go?" he asks.

"I hope you don't mind but the conversation and stuff we talked about came up in the course of the meeting," I say.

He smirks. "I'm not concerned. She has a doctor patient confidentiality agreement and I want you to talk freely to her about anything you want. The good doctor may learn a few things though if you're going to continue seeing her," he says, eyes light with amusement.

I can't help but laugh. "She wants to see me routinely and I agreed to keep my appointments this time. I think we talked more today than during all of our other meetings combined," I say.

"I'm glad you felt comfortable talking to her. She really is known for being the best in her field," he says.

"She thinks I may have post-traumatic stress syndrome," I say, quietly.

He contemplates this a moment before nodding. "I could see how that's likely, Jenny. Seeing Ty was probably a trigger then," he says.

"That's exactly what she said," I say, looking around the enormous living area, out the floor-to-ceiling windows that look over the vast city. Why do I all of a sudden feel so small when I even hear the sound of his name?

Brian's voice brings me back into the present. "Luckily she doesn't know what I want to do to you right now," he says.

"Oh, yeah. What's that?" I ask.

"Oh, I think a little punishment is in order," he says, picking me up. I sink into the firmness of his chest and the beating of his heart. He shifts me in his arms, easily carrying me to his study.

"I've been thinking about you all afternoon, what it would be like to see you stand in front of me while you bare yourself to me. Take off your shirt Jenny, do it now," he says.

My breath hitches, I feel myself moisten and I don't hesitate to slowly drag my sweater over my breasts and then over my head, allowing it to fall to the floor in front of us. He moves my hair to the side and gently kisses the exposed skin of my neck, lingering and sending goose bumps down the sides of each arm.

"You are so sensual," he says, blazing a trail with his tongue down the length of my neck, over my collarbone and letting its heat create a path to my cleavage. The warmth of his breath, mere inches from my nipples turn them hard and erect, wanting his mouth on them. Instead, he traces the delicate white lace covering my skin with his fingers, caressing the same path with his tongue, fueling my need before running one finger over the tip of my extended nipples through the silky material that covers them.

"You're so responsive. I want to see all of you," he says, his eyes glazed with appreciation as he unclips my bra and it slides to the floor. He cups both breasts, gently caressing my nipples, causing my center to clench with desire before he blazes a path with his lips down my stomach. His tongue finds my navel and he pauses to tease and taste, causing my body to tighten in anticipation.

I hold onto the desk behind me for balance. He feels his way back up my length, caressing my calves and thighs, settling on my hips. He inhales me deeply through the thin layer of material. "I can smell your desire, Jenny. It's intoxicating," he says, clasping the waistband of my pants, slowly rolling them along with my panties over my hips and past my thighs before placing them on the growing pile behind him.

"There, let me look at you now," he says, standing back, running his eyes appreciatively over the length of my naked body, my skin heating under the intensity of his gaze. "So I think before we were interrupted we were talking about punishment for kicking me in the balls, stealing my favorite scotch and negotiating over you not telling me you were submissive," he says, walking behind me to the front of his desk.

I hear the drawer open and close behind me and things being shuffled on the desk before he returns to my side. My breath hitches and I feel myself moisten even more. He is fully clothed and his heated gaze makes me feel vulnerable and intensifies my neediness.

"So, would you like me to show you what happens to bad girls that continually break the rules?" he whispers in my ear, gently licking the tender lobe before trailing a path down the expanse of my neck. My nipples tighten and my body clenches as he leaves a mark of heat along the length of my body. He caresses my nipples first with his thumb, then rolls them between his forefinger and thumb causing a slightly painful sensation that immediately causes me to moisten even more.

I moan at the sensation.

"Tell me where you feel that," Brian demands.

"Right in my center, right there," I say.

"Very good," he says, suckling one breast at a time, gently kissing their tips before traveling towards my sensitive navel.

"Tell me how much you like this," he says, softly dipping his tongue into the hole of my navel causing me to squirm.

"I like it very much."

"Does it make you want me to caress this," he says, gently brushing my clit with his thumb.

"Yes, very much," I say, my hips pushing into his finger on their own accord.

"I think I need to check for myself," he says, inserting a finger and then two inside of me and still rubbing my clit with his thumb. My body is on fire and my climax is climbing when he removes his finger and slows his thumb.

"Brian," I moan, so close that I can barely restrain myself from grinding against the heat of his thumb that is just barely caressing me.

"Remember your safe words and use them if you need to. Turn around and bend over for me. I want to see your body spread out over the top of my desk, displayed and ready for me when I punish you," he says huskily.

I look into his eyes and see the same heat of passion I feel before turning around. I lay against the expansive mahogany desk, the coolness of its veneer in direct contrast to the heat of my body.

"You look lovely," he says, running one finger along my

spine before caressing the naked curves of my ass with both hands.

"I'll show you how real punishment works, whatever you want in fact, but if it gets too intense I want you to tell me," he says.

"Sweetheart, I need to hear you," he says, when I don't respond.

"Yes, I'll tell you, Brian. I want to feel it, to know what it's like," I say.

"Hands outstretched, I'm not going to restrain you today. I want you to be in complete control. Hold onto the edge of the desk," he instructs, grazing his hands across my ass cheeks.

My breathing has shallowed and I wait, internally clenching, moist with desire and need, but he is in no hurry, leisurely running a path across my hips and ass with his hands.

"Spanking should only be between two people that trust each other and have conscientiously agreed to the boundaries of what should constitute punishment. Do you trust me to pleasure you, Jenny?" he says.

"Yes, completely."

"Very well, we'll start with ten strikes and I want you to count aloud with me," he says as the first sting of his palm makes contact with my ass. I gasp aloud at the burn. "Count, Jenny," Brian reminds.

"One," I say, before another smack of his hand connects in the same spot, sending a shiver of pain and desire through my body. "Two, three." This time the contact lands just off the spot of the last two, but begins coming slightly faster. My breathing is ragged as I count through the exquisite pain to my ass cheeks and the throbbing delight fanning deep in my center, "four, five, six," I pant.

"Breathe deeply and then count out the last four with me. Now," he instructs and I gulp in a lung full of air. "Exhale and count with me," he says as he connects with the tender underside of my ass cheeks, one after another until we reach ten. The coolness of the desk on the front of my body is in contrast to the heat of my ass. He runs his hands along the length of my body.

"I want to see for myself how wet you are," he says, slipping a finger inside of me and then two. "Oh, Sweetheart you're absolutely soaked," he says, as his zipper comes down and I feel the head of his cock next to me. Tell me what you want now, Jenny."

"You inside of me, deep inside of me," I moan, overcome with the force of desire and need for release as I hear the condom wrapper and feel him pushing into me, rooting himself deeply, pulling my hips toward his as he drives against that special spot, over and over, relentlessly thrusting until I am moaning and right on the brink.

"Come for me," he instructs, pushing us over the edge, allowing wave after wave to consume me before easing out of me and turning me around to take me in his arms as we slowly come down and begin to recover. "Stay here," he says after some time, reaching for the box of tissues, discarding the condom, cleaning himself before gently wiping me and layering kisses along the warmth of my ass.

He pulls me toward him, situating me on the edge of the desk so he can stand between my legs. His eyes capture mine and he pushes the hair out of my eyes before kissing my lips gently. "Come on, let's get you cleaned up," he says, picking me up and carrying me into the shower. He washes my body, paying special attention to my hair, shampooing it before putting a deep conditioner in it and massaging my shoulders under the bubbling suds.

"Did you like it when I spanked your ass?" he asks.

"I don't know how to describe it, yet," I say gently.

FOURTEEN

BRIAN

I **know she was turned on**. I felt her wetness all over me but maybe I pushed things too fast trying to help her overcome her fear and fulfill some deep desire, but I can't tell from her response. I spin her around facing away from me so I can rub her back and run my fingers down her spine. I look at her ass to inspect the damage I've caused. Her cheeks are barely pink, but aside from that, nothing. I take stock in the fact that I took it very easy on her when in reality I wanted to tie her up and be very rough with her, punishing her for all of her mischievous disobedience.

I use the showerhead to rinse the conditioner out of her long brunette tresses and wrap her in a towel from the warming station before handing her one for her hair. She bends upside down and wraps her hair like a turban. My dick twitches at the opportunity to fuck her in that very position.

"Why don't you dry your hair and I'll get us something for dinner," I say, sliding into my lounge pants and heading into the kitchen to avoid the feeling of guilt and shame washing over me. I know she enjoyed it, I heard her moans and felt how wet she was, but damn it, it was just too soon!

I yank open the refrigerator doors looking for whatever Celia has left us to eat, pulling out a saran wrapped pot pie and put three pieces onto a microwavable dish before pouring us each a glass of white wine. I wonder if we will have to go over the three drink rule again and notice that my new bottle of scotch is now locked in the glass cabinet. I chuckle to myself wondering if she'll try to break into that tonight and then shake my head at the thought of how much fun punishing her for such disobedience would be.

The food is still heating when Scottie's ring tone comes through. "This is Brian," I say, hitting the connect button.

"Hey, I've got a little more information."

"Fill me in," I say, taking a sip of my wine.

"I'm still trying to put all the pieces together but Chase knew from what Ty told Jenny that he was funneling money through Torzial, but not from where or for who. I've had a team poring over his accounts and it looks like aside from the sale of information to the pharm companies he was also embezzling money from at least one or two of them, running that money through Torzial and then straight to his account in the Caymans.

"Damn, I figured it was something like that," I say.

"Wish it was that easy, lad. There's every likelihood that Ty was also laundering money for Mancini," he says.

"Fuck, he was laundering money for the mafia through Torzial?" I say.

"Not exactly. Word on the street is that Mancini's been skimming money from the Chicago mafia," Scottie says.

"Fuck me!"

"The day before Ty's hospitalization Chase attended a pharmaceutical meeting with the firm's board. I'd say that Chase was laying the foundation to have Ty sent up the river for embezzlement but Carlos Larussio's brother got to him first trying to pin a phony murder rap on Carlos.

"Did the pharmaceutical companies ever go after him legally?" I ask, muttering under my breath as I pull the hot plate out of the microwave and burn my fingers.

"No, and can you blame them? After what happened to him, they probably wanted to stay as far away as possible so they weren't linked to the assault."

"Yeah, I can't say as I blame them," I say.

"I'm not sure how much you and Chase are talking about the Alfreita situation, but it's gotten a little larger than just him. Carlos has two more brothers and an uncle living in Italy who's not too happy about the plans he's made for the future. We've intercepted communications that confirm the uncle and Alfreita are working together and it may be an attempt to overthrow Carlos."

"Shit, does Chase know that he's caught in the fucking middle of this?" I ask.

"It would appear so my friend. Chase has fallen in love with the only daughter of the biggest mafia boss in America who just happens to be on the bad side of one of the biggest mafia bosses in old world Italy. Couple that with the fact that Dominic Mancini appears to have been funneling the money he skimmed off the Chicago mob into her best friend's business. Word on the street is that shit's about to get ugly," Scottie says.

"Holy shit!" I say.

"For now, keep your lovely nice and safe and let me and my teams work through this. Jenny is also on Alfreita's pick list. She apparently accompanied Kate on a trip to Brazil to meet with Vicenti, the Brazilian cartel leader that Carlos plans to sell his product to," he says.

"Come again, why would she do that?" I say, taking another long pull on my wine.

"She went with Kate to see him after the skirmish in the Caribbean. When the Larussio brother tried to take Carlos and Chase out Jay ended up taking a bullet. Carlos was flown back to a Chicago hospital and Jay was air-evacuated to Brazil. Chase got thrown into the slammer and Kate took things into her own hands. I thought you knew all this," he says.

"Yeah, I know some of it, but Chase never talked about the details and I didn't ask. After the arrest his lawyer hauled me in, told me he had been arrested for a trumped up drug trafficking charge, told me about the shooting and gave me instructions for the company," I say.

"Kate coerced one of Chase's security men into having her flown to Brazil. She went to visit Jay in ICU and then somehow managed to orchestrate a visit with Vicenti to get him to intervene on Chase's behalf. The next day, Chase walked."

"Fuck me! How did you get through Chase's intel and find that out?" I ask.

"We didn't. It's seriously impermeable. We hacked into the surveillance at Vicenti's. I've got another call coming in from intel that I need to take. Talk you to later," he says before disconnecting.

I try to absorb everything that he has told me, but I need to talk to Chase and send a text to Scottie.

Message: Get a hold of Jay and set up a secure call between Chase and me.

Reply: Will do.

FIFTEEN

JENNY

I t's just after seven and I've dried my hair and slipped
into a pale-peach colored lacy nightgown. I'm still having
a difficult time thinking about anything else except the
way Brian spanked and fucked me. The way he punished me
leaves me thinking about kicking him in the balls and stealing
some more of his scotch tonight. It's only been an hour since we
were together but my body is moist just thinking about the way
it felt to get laid across his desk, completely vulnerable, getting
my ass spanked with the palm of his hand.

When I hear Kate's ringtone, I hit the button to connect and
put her on speaker phone. "Hi there," I say.

"Hi yourself. So, are you going to fill me in with what's
going on between you and Brian? I'm dying to find out," she
says, causing my cheeks to flush as Brian walks into the room
carrying a tray with two plates and a glass of wine for each of

us. He levels me with his gaze and I can't help but blush under his scrutiny. He smirks as he sets the tray on the side table and walks into the bathroom closing the door behind him.

"I seriously never thought sex could be this good. God, Kate, how to describe it, like umm, you know, not exactly vanilla," I say quietly so he can't hear me.

"Oh, that kind of stuff," she says, laughing softly and I can just imagine the wide grin on her face.

"The best kind if you ask me," I say.

"Aren't you supposed to be resting, young lady," Kate teases.

"That's all I've been doing. Sleeping, reading, talking. I think that was exactly what I needed," I say in my own defense.

"Well I'm very happy for you. Chase thinks the world of Brian. I'm glad he's been there for you. It sounds like you're doing well," she says.

"Kate, I'm a lot better. I was able to talk to the counselor, really talk to her this time, but I am wondering if I could ask you a favor," I say.

"Anything for you," she says.

"If I transfer all my emails to you, would you be able to manage things for a bit?" I ask.

"Of course, just set up the permissions and I'll sign on a little later. I need to go now, but I'll call you tomorrow," she says, disconnecting as Brian comes out of the bathroom with his wine.

He puts his glass down on the nightstand and settles onto the bed beside me as I get off the phone. "I wasn't trying to eavesdrop, but it was impossible not to hear your conversation. You liked what I did to you?" he says, pushing a long strand of hair out of my face and behind my ear.

"Why would you ask me that? It's like a dream come true, better even," I say, realizing my cheeks are flushed.

His face crinkles in confusion but his bright crystalline blue eyes are alight. "You said you weren't sure how you felt about what we did. I thought it might have been too fast, that it was too much too soon," he says.

"No, actually nothing could be farther from the truth. It was liberating. It's the first time in so long that I felt like I had complete control over everything that was happening and the ability to do what made me feel good, and fuck what anyone else thinks," I say.

"That's my girl," he says, caressing my cheek.

I reach for the glass of wine and take a sip. "In fact, it's got me so worked up I was trying to figure out how to steal another bottle of scotch tonight," I say, winking at him over the rim of my glass.

He smirks and is eyes light up with bemusement. "Oh, you just feel free to sneak into anything off limits that you can."

"That sounds like a challenge I can't refuse," I say.

"Sweetheart, I'm going to test every limit you have but I was serious before. We need to go slow," he says, kissing my hair.

"That's what safe words are for, right?" I say and grin at the look of genuine surprise on his face.

"Eat your dinner before I decide there's no time like the present for a little training," he says, settling the tray across my lap. I am so hungry that I nearly devour the large slice of home-made chicken pot pie. It has roasted chicken, cubed potatoes, carrots, celery, and corn combined with garlic, black pepper, and thyme wrapped into a deliciously flaky crust.

"This is absolutely delicious," I say, finishing my slice. He has a few mouthfuls of his second piece left and feeds me the last two bites with his fork. "I love watching your lips wrap around that lucky little fork," he says, huskily.

"Give me some more wine and I'll wrap them around your cock," I say, relishing in the sharp intake of his breath.

"You get my cock when you've earned it. Right now, you're causing me distress and worry. I want nothing more than to spank your ass with my bare hands and to feel your firm cheeks warming underneath them while you squirm on my lap," he says.

The moisture pools at my center and I have a hard time looking up, but he captures my chin and forces me to gaze into his crystal blue eyes. "Tell me how that makes you feel," he says, setting the tray with our plates onto the side table, pushing me back onto the bed, and then rolling me so I'm facing him.

"I love it. The way you talk to me makes me hot. I always dreamed that someday I'd find someone that liked things like this. Even thought of going to clubs to find someone but they're strangers. Maybe I'm old-fashioned, but I just need the connection with someone that really cares about me, you know," I say.

"Clubs aren't all bad," he says, kissing my forehead before sliding off the bed. I watch as he walks away from me anticipating a surprise, a toy or something, but he turns toward me and the look on his face is hard to discern.

"You've had an incredibly long day. Get a good night's sleep. We'll talk in the morning," he says, before he walks right out the door and closes it behind him.

What the hell just happened? I replay our conversation over and over. He told me I should open up. I was sharing with him and then he leaves. I must have offended him with the club remark. Maybe that's what he's into, getting it on with strangers. Now that I think about it, it makes perfect sense. He would have fucked me the first night I met him if I hadn't gotten freaked out.

It's still very early and I'm sure he'll tell me what's on his mind when he's ready. I do want more wine though, and go out to the kitchen in search of it. He is nowhere in sight and I decide to take the chilled bottle with me back to his room. The wine door is still unlocked so I tuck a couple bottles under my arm, carting them back to the bedroom with me, anticipating a delicious punishment.

I pour myself a glass of wine and sign onto emails responding to most of them, copying the managers they impact along with Chase, Brian, and Kate so she can take the information and manage it where applicable. After a couple hours and bottles of wine I am finished, wiped out from the emotions of the day and the overwhelming amount of requests for consulting advice coming in from all over the country.

In the morning the sun is shining brightly through the windows and I cover my alcohol- hazed eyes in protest as I try to clear my brain. I glance at Brian's side of the bed and realize it's been left untouched. I don't know why the realization that he left me in his bed alone bothers me. I should be happy that I slept through the night on my own. I brush my teeth before pinning my hair up and head to the shower, letting the spray of the rainforest showerhead sprinkle over my head and shoulders and down my back. Another twenty self-indulgent minutes later and I feel relaxed and wide awake. I apply a light moisturizer onto my towel-dried skin before slipping into my clothes and heading into the kitchen.

"Good morning," Celia says, hunched over the countertop, reading something.

"Morning," I say, feeling suddenly shy about what she must think about my presence in their home.

"Would you like a cup of coffee? I just brewed a fresh pot unless you prefer a K-Cup," she says, pointing towards the assortment on the counter.

"I had a caramel yesterday but only because Brian didn't make the real stuff," I say as she nods.

"A girl after my own heart," she says, pouring me a freshly brewed cup.

"Do you use creamer? I purchased several, including

caramel. I noticed that seemed to be your favorite flavor," she says warmly.

"Mmm, caramel creamer would be amazing. Do you know where Brian is?" I ask, glancing around.

"He was up early, took in the stocks and productivity reports, got a workout in and left. Hard to say where that young man is," she says, shaking her head.

"French toast?" she asks, pulling a plate out of the oven. "It's my famous banana nut recipe," she says.

"Yes, please. It smells great," I say, practically salivating and digging into the meal as soon as it's placed before me. "We had a piece of your pot pie last night. It was excellent, too," I say.

"Glad you enjoyed it," she says, cleaning up in the kitchen before heading back to her office.

I am not sure what to do with myself after breakfast and sign onto email. My inbox has filled back up and I shake my head at the magnitude of all the requests for bids and other things that people are requesting. I sign off knowing that Kate has everything in complete control and that I've assured Dr. Werther that I will take at least a couple weeks off.

I take another self-guided tour of the penthouse. The home is vast and makes me feel small and even more alone. I don't have a clue what to do with myself except work and that's off the table for now. I head into his library, impressed again at his hardcover collection, selecting a classic and settling into a comfy armchair to pass the time before he comes home and I can find out why he left so abruptly. With every hour left alone my frustration grows. Pompous ass! After all his talk about opening up he sure couldn't do the same. If I pissed him off, why not tell me, at least say something? It is late afternoon and I am still fuming when Kate calls.

"Hi there. It's your daily pain in the ass," she says.

I smile, wishing she weren't so far away and I could reach out and hug her. "What are you doing?" I ask.

"Actually, just got done with email from the Prestian Corp account and talked to Mom for a little while. How are you doing?" she asks.

I feel bad that I've now given her even more to do, but keep it to myself. Hopefully Dr. Werther won't want to keep me from work for too long. "I'm good." I also don't tell her that Brian isn't talking to me. One minute we're about ready to have hot sex and the next minute he walked right out on me and hasn't talked to me since. I listen to her summaries of a few accounts, but I barely hear what she's saying. I know she's got it under control and after a short time we disconnect.

The more I think about Brian the madder I become. I don't want to stay here, won't stay here. I skim through his closet and can't help but smile remembering how Kate snuck by her security earlier in the year. I slip out of my clothes and let them pool to the floor, left only in my thong.

I slide one of his black Armani suits off the hanger and pull on a pair of matching pants. I then select one of his crisp white dress shirts and button it up, tucking the excess material into the pants before choosing a belt from several on the wall. I slide it into the belt loops and tighten. I shuffle into the bathroom and pull out a pair of scissors and poke a few extra holes in the belt and cinch it again, folding the excess material over the belt. The jacket goes on disguising the ridiculous fit of the pants and I glance down, trying to figure out how the shoes will ever fit. Socks! A couple of them tucked into the tops of the shoes will work perfectly! I twist my hair into a messy bun and pull a hat off a shelf in the closet and place it slant-wise over my head, giggling. No one will ever know it's me.

I peel out of his clothes, attempting to keep them as wrinkle free as possible while packing them into my laptop bag. I put my own clothes back on and text Matt.

Message: I need to see my counselor.

Reply: I'll clear it with Brian.

Message: I can't wait. I'm leaving now.

I walk out the door shrugging off warnings from the security men who follow me into the elevator. This is not going to be as easy as I thought. The doors open to the reception area.

"I need a limo to Dr. Werther. Can you arrange that while I go to the bathroom? I'm not feeling well," I say, rushing past them to the restroom.

SIXTEEN

BRIAN

I **am working; it's what** I do when I'm not in the middle of an acquisition or in the company of a woman for the night. If they come too close, I turn them loose and that's what I need to do with Jenny. Relationships are not my fucking thing. As if on cue a text message from Sasha appears on my cell phone.

Message: I miss you. Any chance you're in the mood, Lover boy?

I've done everything possible to let her know I'm no longer interested. I try my best not to recall the three times I used her body for my perverse pleasure.

Reply: It's over, Sasha.

Once they know who I am every fucking one of them wants a relationship just like all the women that used to fuck my dad down in the pool house when he thought no one was around to see his indiscretions. They didn't give a shit about him, just what he could buy them. How many of them had penthouses and cars provided by him to ensure they'd drop their little panties as soon as he called. How many years did my mom look the other way just to retain the status she had become accustomed to in life? There's a reason I don't let anyone close and while I bent my rules with Sasha slightly, Jenny has managed to annihilate any semblance of order in my carefully laid out structure. Hit 'em and quit 'em. No one in my bed two times in a row, no unprotected sex, no contact the next day, no fucking chance of developing feelings for someone.

I glance down at the incoming text from Scottie.

Message: Brian, Jenny took off. The guys are looking for her, reviewing surveillance cameras as we speak.

Reply: Fuck! Find her!

I punch Chase's phone number and he answers immediately. "This is Brian, Jenny took off," I say.

"I just got word, too. Jay just sent through a text to let me know. Why would she leave knowing the danger? Katarina just talked to her an hour or so ago and thought she seemed fine," Chase says.

I refrain from telling him what a fucked up asshole I am. Instead I read him what Scottie has texted me. "They think they found her on camera. She went into the bathroom and came out dressed as a guy," I say, my jaw clenching as I open up the picture of her in my Armani suit and one of the old hats my father used to wear. Well played, Sweetheart.

"Damn it, that's the second time that's worked. Katarina did the same thing earlier in the year," Chase says.

"You think she helped Jenny out?" I ask.

"No, she would have insisted she come here if she was leaving your place."

"Just got a text from Matt. He's got her." Chase says.

"Where is she?" I demand.

"She went home."

"Damn stubborn woman. She's going to get herself killed!"

"What the hell is going on with you two, Brian?"

"None of your fucking business and by the way, what the hell is going on with Alfreita and why did Jenny and Kate go to see Vicenti earlier in the year?" I demand.

"The Alfreita thing is almost over. I don't want you or Jenny involved," he says.

"We're already fucking involved, Chase. They could have taken us out the other night," I say.

There is a heavy sigh on the other end. "When I was arrested, Katarina persuaded the security team to take her to Brazil. She found out Jay had kept surveillance tapes that cleared my name and that I wasn't talking because it might have incriminated the Larussios."

I let out a quiet whistle. "Damn, you mean if you had come clean Carlos would have been indicted?" I ask, knowing Chase's dad and Carlos go way back.

"No, Tony, but I didn't know his brother was acting on his own at the time. I wasn't about to bring trouble to the family doorstep. Hang tight Brian. It's going to be over shortly. Things are starting to fall into place," Chase says.

"That doesn't help the situation with Jenny. She's not staying at her place by herself."

"Good. There's one more thing you should know. Ty sent Jenny a message but she hasn't seen it. Katarina's been taking care of her mail and showed it to me. I'll send a copy to your email. Let me know when you have it," Chase says.

"I'm reading it now," I say between clenched teeth.

You appeared a little ashen at last evening's festivities. Perhaps a little too much to drink or were you thinking about something in particular? Perhaps the special night we shared? I sincerely hope that is the case and if so that you continue to dream about that every night until I can repay you for all the joy you have brought me and we can be together again. Until then your secret about Torzial is safe with me.

Yours always, Ty

"I'm going to get her and keep Matt out of my fucking way. She's coming home with me," I say, disconnecting as I take off and text Wes to have the car pulled around.

SEVENTEEN

JENNY

I should feel remorse, or something close to it, lying and deceiving the people who have been protecting me for hours on end, but I don't feel anything except a strong need to take back control of my life. I walk out of the bathroom and keep my eyes on the exit, moving straight ahead. I push through the door and see a limo waiting and a couple taxis sitting idle right down the street. I walk right past the limo and open the back door of one of the cabs as I reach it.

"Waiting for someone or can you take me somewhere?" I ask.

"Hop in," he says and I give him my address. I am anxious to see my new condo now that it has all of my own furniture in it.

The driver navigates the heavy Chicago traffic like he's been doing it all his life. I take the hat off and pull my hair out of the scrunchy, shaking it loose, letting it fall over my shoulders and breasts.

"Shit, you one of those hot girls that dresses up like a dude?" the guys says, glancing away as my eyes catch his watching me in the rearview mirror.

"Pretend you didn't see me if anyone asks," I say, settling back into the seat as he winds himself around town and towards my apartment.

"You got it," he says.

"How long have you been driving?" I ask to pass the time.

"Just about ten years. It's taken me that long to save enough to start my own company. I'm going into business for myself at the end of the month, starting out with a few Cadillacs and a couple of limos," he says proudly.

"Very nice. You have business cards?" I ask.

"Sure do," he says, handing me one over the seat.

"If I come into contact with anyone that needs a ride I'll be sure to share it with them," I say, recalling my earlier years just trying to get word out about my own business.

"Well, in that case take a few," he says, handing me a stack and grinning widely.

"Don't mind if I do," I say, tucking them into Brian's suit pocket and handing him a wad of bills as we pull up to my condo. The cash is more than enough to cover the fare along with a very generous tip.

"Thanks for the ride. It was nice to meet you Sal," I say, getting out of the car and closing the door behind me.

I walk into the complex and head to the elevators determined to get a grip on my life, roll back to the time when I was just starting out, had a few dollars from my father, and a dream and hard fucking work was the only thing that mattered. I didn't depend on anyone, just myself. In fact, I had too many people depending on me to let them down and I still do. I need to get over this pity party and take control of my life again. It happened, it's over, life goes on. I am riding in the elevator to one of the top floors, a sign of my success in this massive city. I don't need Brian to make me feel better, I just need to pull myself up by the bootstraps, brush off and get back on the horse of life. Fuck him and fuck Ty for making me a victim and fuck me for letting him. No fucking more!

I push the key code into my new apartment, letting myself in and glancing around. While the views certainly don't compare to Brian's, I love the windows that allow me a real-life look onto the sprawling lakefront and Chicago sky-rises, and the contemporary way the designers have created the space. White and pewter cabinets and solid birch wood flooring throughout.

The knock on the door pulls me out of my reverie and I wonder with annoyance if the bellman downstairs is looking for another tip for bringing my mail up right away.

I look into the peephole and open the door with a sigh. Matt is standing there, looking thoroughly annoyed. "I was worried about you," he says, pushing the door aside.

"Well, no need. As you can see I'm just fine," I say.

"You know Alfreita's out there. We need you where you're

safe," he says.

"I'm not going back to Brian's," I say.

"Then let me take you to Chase's," he counters, not even asking me why I don't want to stay with Brian anymore.

"No, I'm staying here, in my apartment, in my own corner of the world. I am tired of being afraid, tired of running. You can stay or you can go, but I am not leaving my home," I say.

His jaw tightens. "Okay, let me head down and give Chase and Brian a call while I get my things. They're not going to be happy about it, but they'll be glad you're safe and Alfreita doesn't have you. I'll leave a guard by the elevator while I'm gone," he says, closing the door behind him.

"Well, well, well… wasn't that the sweetest fucking thing I've ever heard."

I whirl around and Ty is standing behind me. A scream tries to escape, but he's too fast. My mouth is covered with a cloth and he tapes it shut. Before I know what's happening he's hauling me into the bedroom by my hair and pushing me roughly onto the bed. "You enjoyed it so much the last time I think a redo is in order," he says, sneering at me as he pulls my hands above my head, tying them with an abrasive rope. I jerk against them but the tightness and coarseness begin to cut into my delicate flesh almost immediately.

He's sneering at me from swollen bruised lips and is missing a front tooth. "I thought I'd have all afternoon to upload the files that will prove you were laundering money without my knowledge. Imagine my surprise when I heard your door opening. I was going to visit you later when you got done shacking up with lover boy, but it looks like we can kill two birds with one stone," he says as he takes hold of one of my feet, easily capturing it and securing it to the bedpost.

He is intent on what he is doing and so am I. I breathe deeply, inhaling and exhaling. My right foot, the one that's been locked knee to chest is waiting for that perfect moment and when it comes I take it, driving my foot through the air with as much force as I can muster. It connects with its target. My angle drives upward smashing into his nose, connecting hard and he's suddenly screaming in pain.

"You broke my fucking nose you bitch," he's shouting and one look at his face tells me the bone has been shoved up into his sinus cavities. He's walking aimlessly around the room yelling obscenities and blood is gushing everywhere.

"Fucking bitch!" I didn't hit him hard enough. I should have shoved the nose bone right into his brain but I didn't succeed. He's still very much alive, his nose is dripping blood and his eyes are menacing as he walks toward me and backhands me across the face. "That was a big fucking mistake you little cunt," he says, slapping me again and again.

"You're going to wish you hadn't done that," he sneers, walking to the end of the bed, roughly capturing the foot that just connected with his face. He painfully tightens his grip and I grimace at the intensity of his hold as he ties it to the bedpost. "There, all spread out for me like the fucking little whore you are. Now the fun begins. I think we'll start by cutting off these clothes. I just hope I'm able to see well enough with all the blood running down my face and don't accidentally slip and cut something important," he jeers.

I should be scared, I should be freaking the fuck out but I'm calm as I catch a glimpse of Brian walking up behind him and look Ty right in the eyes as something hits him solidly on the head. He falls forward but Brian pulls him off of me, spinning him around and slams his fist into Ty's face repeatedly until finally Matt pulls him away.

"Enough, get the hell out of here and let us deal with this mess," Matt says.

Brian begins untying me while Matt deals with Ty. "She's not staying here," Brian says, scooping me into his arms.

"I can walk," I protest and he doesn't say a word, just glares at me and doesn't put me down until we're in the back of his limo and even then he only lets me far enough out of his arms to buckle me in, but then pulls me back into the warmth and protection of his arms. His hands are bleeding and I take one in my own. "Thank you for what you did," I say.

He doesn't respond but squeezes me tighter as we navigate across the city traffic back to his place. His cell phone vibrates almost constantly all the way across town, but he continuously ignores it and when we pull up outside of his complex he steps out and leans down to pick me up.

"I can manage, Brian," I say, but he shakes his head and places his hands under my knees, easily lifting me while I cling to his neck and burrow my face into his chest. We are surrounded by security guards as we enter the private elevator that opens into his penthouse suite.

He finally puts me down when we reach the bathroom. It's only now that I see the large amount of blood he has all over his suit, not just his hands, but everywhere and realize that it's smeared onto my clothing as well. He begins removing his clothing and it feels like a slow motion action film but I can't turn away. He is all male as he strips to his underwear, removing his bloodied suit, white dress shirt, and tie before undressing me slowly, taking my hand and leading me into the shower. He turns the water on and lets it run over us, just holding me tight for a while before he lifts my chin so that my eyes meet his.

"I'm so fucking sorry I left you alone. I'm so fucking sorry," he says, bending down and kissing me lightly on the lips, gently caressing the tender bruising skin of my cheek.

"It's not your fault," I say, reaching for his bloodied knuckles, but he turns me around to face the stone wall of the shower.

"Stay still, let me take care of you," he says, adjusting the shower stream to wet my body before moving it to cascade down my back as he rubs the mango scented shampoo into my hair and massages my scalp, working his way slowly down the back of my head and neck.

"It feels so good," I say, pushing into the feel of his hands as they adjust my head to rinse the soap from my hair.

"There, time for the conditioner," he says, slathering the silky cream onto my scalp, and gently massaging it through my hair. I love that he's taking care of me and can't help the sound that escapes me as he rubs the lather lower, caressing the bottom of my scalp, and kneads the top of my neck with his hands.

"I love it when you purr for me Sweetheart," he says, letting the warmth of the water cascade over me, rinsing me completely.

When I come out of the bathroom he's in bed, sitting up against the headboard, just watching me, his laptop in front of him untouched. I slide in next to him and haul the sheet and blanket with me.

"I can't stand that the fucker had his hands on you and that it was my fault."

"How do you think this was remotely your responsibility?" I ask.

"Letting you out of my sight, leaving you alone," he grinds out.

"Brian, I'm a grown woman. I don't recall asking if I could leave. I wanted to try and take back control of my life. I know that if you hadn't showed up it would have been much worse, but I didn't cower and I stood up for myself."

"You fucked him up good, but it doesn't change the fact that I wish I hadn't left you alone," he says.

"Why did you, Brian? I have no idea what I said that caused you to walk out when we were about ready to have sex. Look at everything that I've shared with you. If you're into club scenes we should talk about it. I'm open to new experiences and I can go with you and take a look around," I say even though the thought of seeing or having sex in public is not very appealing.

He puts his laptop on the nightstand and repositions me so I'm straddling him. His eyes have darkened and he's looking at me intently. "Listen to me. It has nothing to do with nightclubs but you're not that far off. It's about lifestyle. I'm not a long term romance kind of guy. I'm more of a hit it and quit it guy," he says as I cringe.

"Hit it and quit it, like fuck them, breakfast in bed and then so long, see you and never call them back?" I ask.

"More like fuck them, say good night, never get their number and most definitely never call them back, with few exceptions to that rule," he says.

"Like seriously only one night stands," I say, mulling this over.

"Yes, with a couple exceptions," he repeats.

"So you walked out on me because I was one of the exceptions and we were breaking your rules?"

"Fucking for me isn't about caring or feeling, it's a basic need like water and food. I'm a man."

"Oh, now the light comes on," I say, trying my best to keep the tinge of sarcasm out of my voice. "I pushed your rules button when I said something about you caring for me. Well, news flash. Most men don't usually fly someone in trouble to their home, protect them and make love to them if they don't care just a little bit. At least in my world, but please feel free to educate me if I'm off base," I say.

"You most definitely are. You can't grow up the way I did, in a life of opulence and unbelievable wealth, watching young glassy-eyed whores fawn all over your father and the pain in your mothers eyes, always looking the other way to maintain her own status, or the girls, endless scores of girls, crawling all over me once they figured out who I was and understood how many dollar signs come with the name. It taints you and couple that with the fact my sexual appetites aren't everyone's cup of tea. It is what it is," he says, shrugging.

"That's unfortunate, but there have to be many successful businessmen who have girls after them for their money. I'm not saying it's right, but why would you let it affect you like this?"

"For fuck's sake as close as I was to my parents they wanted to marry me off to some tycoon's daughter to merge the global steel businesses. No thank you, hit 'em and quit 'em," he says.

"Well for the record, I'm not looking for a relationship. As you know, the last one didn't end so well, but I'd love one more ride on your cock if that's not breaking the rules too much," I say, trying to avoid his eyes so he can't see the pain his words cause.

He looks at me intensely and I watch as a myriad of emotions wash over his eyes but it's hard to discern any meaning. "You've been through hell and back. I don't want to hurt you," he says, caressing the most swollen and painful area of my face with the lightest of touches.

"You're not going to hurt me, I want this," I say.

I watch as the storm plays out in his crystalline eyes and he shifts me before rolling on a condom. He pauses, as if waiting for permission and I moan with anticipation right before he lifts me, slipping his hard length inside of me, slowly controlling my movement, up and down. I place my hands on his shoulders and he begins swiveling my hips, forcing his cock to hit that special place that he already knows so well. I rock back and forth and moan as he plays, slow and then fast, gaining momentum, pulling me down and pushing against that special little button deep inside of me. The rush is building fast and he must feel it, he speeds our intensity, pushing us both over the edge as we release together and I collapse on his chest.

When I wake the bed is empty and I head to the bathroom, shower, get ready for the day, and head into the kitchen. Celia is already there making breakfast and Brian is nowhere in sight.

"Where's Brian?" I ask.

She points down the hall. "Working in his study today," she says as she pours me a cup of coffee and takes the creamer out of the refrigerator.

"Has he eaten, yet?" I ask.

"Hours ago. What would you like? I still have some blueberry muffins left," she says.

"That would be amazing!" I say.

"Perfect, I'll bring them to you with coffee shortly," she says as I turn towards his office.

He looks disgruntled at first but his features soften somewhat as he sees it's me. He places the caller on speaker as Celia follows me in with a tray and sets it on the desk.

"Thanks Celia," I say as he reaches for the coffee, pouring us each a cup.

"Most welcome. Let me know if you need anything else," she says, closing the door behind her as she leaves.

"Gentlemen, let's debrief again at noon. Scottie can you set up the line?" he says, before disconnecting and looking back down at his laptop.

"So did Chase hire Scottie to take care of your security needs like Jay does for him? I don't know how I'll ever repay him for having Matt stay with me the last few months," I say, trying to break through the silence.

His jaw tightens. "Jenny, Scottie is on my payroll, not Prestian Corps," he says.

"Really, you hired someone outside of Jay to help with all the stuff going on? I thought he was working for Chase. Did you talk to Matt about it?"

"Jenny, my security team has been working with Jay and Matt from the time you originally went missing," he says.

"I had no clue. Thank you for hiring them," I say, realizing this conversation is getting us nowhere closer to discussing our relationship or lack of one.

He flips the lid of his Mac down and looks up at me. "I

didn't hire them specifically for you. I have my own round-the-clock security team. My parents are deceased and left me an empire at a very early age. Security is a necessity," he says.

"I'm so sorry for your loss, Brian. I wasn't aware," I say, taking a sip of my coffee.

"You really don't know who I am, do you?" he asks, watching me warily.

"Of course I do. You're the famous COO of Prestian Corp rumored to make men sweat at the negotiation table. You're best friends with Chase, best man at his wedding and you are very forward with women. You like to make their panties wet, and then fuck them with no breakfast or follow-up call," I say, smiling at the amusement in his eyes and upturned quirk of his lips.

"Jenny, I've worked for Prestian Corp the last five years because after I graduated with my masters I wanted to learn practical application of global business from the best. Chase Prestian is the best and he learned from the very best, his father. My parents were Carolyn and Gregory Carrington," he says.

"It couldn't have been easy to lose both of your parents at an early age, and I'm sorry but those names don't ring any bells," I say.

He shakes his head. "Son of a bitch," he mumbles.

"Well, don't just leave me hanging, apparently there's a juicy story I've missed somehow. I blame Kate. You simply can't rely on best friends to divulge their boyfriend's best friend's secrets anymore," I say, dramatically.

He smirks. "You're going to find out soon enough. I am the one and only heir to the Carrington Steel Empire and my internship with Chase will be done at the end of the month. I've already taken over Carrington Steel but wanted to make sure the new COO for Prestian Corp was settled in before I left. Scottie is the head of the global security team for Carrington."

"Carrington Steel? Shit, Brian. Everyone knows Carrington Steel. I recall reading about their portfolio in some of Chase's information. I never made the connection though. I mean, how would I, you worked for Chase," I say.

"So, would you like to start over Ms. Torzial? I'm Brian Carrington, owner of the largest steel industry on the globe and I would love to get into your panties and I know whether you like what I have to say or not, I'll get laid because no woman can pass up the chance at the opportunity to snag someone with that much money," he says, smirking.

"I'd love to start over, Mr. Carrington. I'm Ms. Torzial, and my panties were incredibly wet for you the night we met. I could have easily gone home with you if I weren't so screwed up from a past relationship. Then you rescued me, kept me safe, and introduced me to the best sex of my life. I started to like you and even contemplated what a relationship with you would be like but then I learned what a pompous, arrogant, womanizer you are and suddenly, I find myself turned the fuck off and no longer interested," I say, striding right out of the room and slamming the office door behind me.

EIGHTEEN

BRIAN

Fuck me! She just walked right out the door and slammed the fucker, too. I try to recall if anyone has ever done that to me. Nope, I can't remember one time in my life when a girl got upset with me, or even tried to call me out on any of my shit. They were always too busy trying to make me happy. "Yes, Brian, anything you say, Brian," eyelashes batting and little lips pouting. And the amount of fake orgasms from these frigid little money mongers. Didn't their mamas teach them that men can tell? That a man can feel the moisture of a woman's real desire soaking and coating them, the feel of a clenching pussy that's about ready to explode, giving a guy just the right amount of time to bring her over the edge.

I think back to last night and the way Jenny's pussy was gushing all over me. Damn she was hot and when I felt her tightening around me she was already clawing at the back of my neck, desperate to come all over my balls. That was my cue to ram it home and bring us both over the edge.

Shit, I should go find her and fuck her some more, get her out of my system, but I already know that won't work because *this* is not like *that*. All the other relationships have been pure sex. No intellectual or emotional chemistry, no one and I mean no one in my home or bed, no one that I'm protecting or would pummel a guy for and according to the text messages accumulated in my inbox I have done more than that. She seriously didn't know who I was— what a total mind fuck!

I finish a few things for work and continue to take pulls on my coffee before I give up and go in search of this woman that I would love nothing more than to put over my knee and spank until her ass is bright red. Maybe that's all I need. I've been walking on egg shells with her because of what she's been through. Yes, that's it. Spank her again, maybe a few times and get her right the fuck out of my system. It seems like a good plan and my cock twitches its agreement until I walk into my bedroom, the place where no woman but her has ever been.

She's on my bed, curled up with my pillow, holding onto it for dear life, wearing my t- shirt and crying. Long, drawn out sobs racking her tiny little body like I've hurt her worse than anyone could and I know better than that or at least that's what I think. I can't stand that she's hurting because of me and shut the creaking door behind me.

She looks up and seeing it's me buries her head in my pillow. "Please just go away. I understand your desire not to get close to anyone and I will respect that," she says, trying to hide her sobs.

She has gone through hell and back and still wanted me, well at least until I pushed her away yet again, crying over me instead of all the injustice and hell that she's gone through. That fucking kills me and I find myself pulling her off of my pillow and onto my chest. She finds my heartbeat and burrows her face right there, and it's then that I know if I didn't the first time she sassed me that I want this woman for my very own.

I pull her so close that I might squash the breath right out of her and lift her chin, capturing her lips with a passion I've never felt before, relishing the realization that she wants me, just me. I'm soon peeling her clothes off along with my own. I want her as close to me as possible, no barriers between us, and as soon as I lay us down, both nude, she finds that spot and burrows in, her wet eyelashes drying on my chest as her sobs start to subside.

She is mystifying to me. "I'm sorry," I say, rocking her against my body. She doesn't say a word, just hugs me tighter to her small frame until the sobbing finally stops. I don't know how long I've been holding her when her breathing patterns change. In surprise, I realize she's sleeping. The only time she seems to fall asleep is when she's in my arms and that right there is more fucking powerful than sealing another global deal, buying out a competitor, negotiating the highest price— of all the things I do, this is the best. She feels safe and can sleep and I feel like a fucking king.

I can't take my eyes off of her. What the hell am I going to do with her? I'm not relationship material. I haven't taken a woman on a date in years, and even that was arranged for a social function. I cringe at the memory, just barely adults by law and thrown together in hopes the relationship would move quickly and we would consummate wedding vows, swiftly ensuring Carrington Steel and Coriander Metals took over the globe. Well, thank you mommy and daddy, but I've managed to do that without the help of little miss— shit, I can't even remember her name— oh, yes, Tiffany.

I reluctantly resign myself to letting her rest and getting some work done this afternoon and leave her a note to let her know to meet me for dinner and that I will be working until then. It is almost six when I head into the dining room expecting to see Jenny, but instead I'm met by two empty place settings and Celia.

"Where's Jenny?" I ask as she places a tray with three covered dishes of food onto the table.

"I took her a salad for lunch when she woke up but after that she was busy working on the phone and computer most of the day. She was in the pool for a while before she came upstairs to shower," she says.

"I mean now. Where is she now," I say and I don't know why not knowing exactly where she is when she's supposed to be here with me sets my nerves on edge.

"Give her a few minutes. She'll be here shortly," Celia says, turning to head back into the kitchen. I shrug out of the suit jacket I put on for the last video conference and pour myself a glass of wine, but turn as I sense her presence.

She is wearing a long emerald green evening dress that hugs her delectable curves, showing off her firm tits and cinching to embrace her narrow waist before flowing elegantly down to her four-inch silver sandals. Her dark hair has been curled and cascades over her shoulders and she's applied a deep gloss to those candy cane colored lips of hers. Fuck me!

"You look absolutely gorgeous," I say, drinking her in.

"Thank you," she says and there's that demure little look that makes my dick twitch and my heart skip a beat.

I kiss her lightly on the lips. "Have a seat and I'll pour you a glass of wine," I say, sliding her chair out and getting her settled in before heading to the bar. Celia returns and uncovers the dishes, releasing the smells of the garlic and mushroom flavored pot roast and parmesan crusted potatoes, and serves our meal before leaving again.

"Where were you all day?" she asks, after taking a few bites.

"I had quite a few overseas calls that I took from my study," I say, giving her a rundown of all the latest Prestian Corp developments that may impact Torzial while we eat our meal.

"I hope you don't mind but I used the library for a makeshift office. The views are amazing," she says.

"They are and I don't mind at all. I heard you also enjoyed the pool," I say.

"Back to stalking?" she inquires, giving me that sassy little look over her wine glass.

"That's not likely to change, Sweetheart," I say, coming around to her seat and lifting her.

She shifts in my arms, craning her neck to look at me. I capture her lips, gently at first, but as she opens to me and my willpower to go slow with her diminishes, I kiss her with a fever that takes even my breath away. "I'm sorry I was such an ass, am such an ass," I say.

She puts her forefinger on my lips, shushing me. "It's okay," she says, kissing my lips as we reach the bedroom. I deliberately let her slide down my body until her feet touch the ground before slowly unfastening the dress and leaving her beautifully naked in nothing but her four- inch heels. She might have submissive preferences in the bedroom, but she knows what she wants and I don't know how the hell I've become that, but that's exactly what I want to be. I kiss her and lay her onto her back on my bed. "Don't move or make a sound. If you want me to stop anything that I'm doing all you have to do is tell me, okay?" I ask.

She nods her agreement and although I would normally demand a yes sir, I allow it as consent.

I know how turned on she is because when I kiss her little ears and suck the side of her neck she fucking starts to purr. I want to mark this woman. Never once has that crossed my mind before. Leaving my mark on someone is not part of my rules. Why, when I discard them the next day? But, that is what I fully intend to do. She is mine and I intend to mark her as such.

My cock twitches in anticipation, listening to the little

sounds she makes. She mewls as I suck her soft creamy skin and the way her body arches to meet mine makes my dick want to explode. I slide my finger over her slit and it's hot, the heat coming off of her is intense, but it's nothing compared to inside. I've barely touched her and she's not only slick and wet but she's creamy. Her pre-cum has created this delectable little dessert at the center of her core just for me.

My lips travel down her body, suckling her collarbone, my tongue trailing across the swell of her breast lightly biting her nipples as I make my way south. My tongue teases her, swirling around her mound, licking the corners and creases where her luscious little thighs meet that delicious center. In no time at all, my tongue is buried in honey of the sweetest kind.

Her thighs clench and that's my cue. I find her little nub and rub my tongue over it, and she purrs as I take it between my lips and suck. Her thighs press my head between her legs like a vice and her hands are holding the back of my neck steady. It turns me on that she knows what she likes and I suck harder, thrusting two fingers into her soaking pussy, curling them. I know exactly where her special little spot is and I find it quickly. The combination of my fingers and tongue are too much and she's panting, moaning and coming all over my tongue.

I lap it up; I can't get enough and push her legs up higher. I want to pound her and then flip her over and spank her little ass until its rosy red. I want to hear her beg for me to fuck her and then come all over the perfect little ass that's all mine and that's exactly what I do until we are completely sated and I have her curled into the crook of my arm and she is resting peacefully.

My cell phone vibrates and I pick it up, glancing at the message. Scottie letting me know Ty just got out of surgery. They had to surgically remove the bone Jenny shoved so far up his sinus cavity that it almost killed him. My chest expands with the pride I feel for her.

I ease her sleeping frame onto the pillow and push her hair out of her eyes before I crawl out of bed and slide into my lounge pants and head into the living room. I pour myself a scotch and sink into the leather couch watching the glowing embers of the fireplace while I skim through emails.

A Skype message comes up and I sigh. Sasha. I make a note to have Scottie block her ability to text and Skype me in the morning, but for now it's time to put this to rest. I click on the icon and her face and voice appear on the screen. Her attempt at seduction is obvious, with a see- through red lacy teddy that exposes her erect nipples.

"Hello lover boy," she says in her thick Russian accent.

"Sasha, I thought I made myself pretty clear."

"Oh, don't be like that lover. I'll only be in the United States for a couple more weeks. I thought we could spend time enjoying each other until then. I even purchased some new toys," she says, holding up handcuffs and a riding crop. It is silver handled and has a square rubber paddle attached. My cock stiffens as I look at it, because at this very moment in time I know exactly what I want to do with it. It's the perfect size to spank Jenny's little pussy with.

"Are you listening to me lover boy?" Sasha is saying and I glance back at the screen and she's pulled the top of her bodice down, leaving those perfect tits and nipples on display for me.

"Sasha, we had a great time but I told you, we're through. Please don't contact me again," I say, hitting the disconnect button.

I feel her behind me before I see her. I turn and she is looking at the image of Sasha that hasn't yet disappeared. Her tits are on display and she's dangling handcuffs in one hand and holding the riding crop in the other. I'm sure it all looks pretty fucking incriminating, but I don't apologize. I've done nothing wrong, but her face has this sort of glazed look and for a moment I wonder if I've lost her again.

"Jenny," I start, but she picks that moment to turn and walk out of the room, then I hear her slamming my fucking bedroom door.

NINETEEN
JENNY

I wake to the darkened room with just the city lights shining in. I glance at the clock and realize I've been asleep for just a couple hours. I stretch, deliciously sore from our romp and I can barely get it out of my head. I lost track of the orgasms and the way he spanked my ass was amazing. I blush as I feel myself moistening just at the mere thought.

I go in search of Brian, wearing nothing, knowing Celia is not around and find him sitting by the fireplace talking to someone on his computer. I walk closer and it's hard not to stare at the beautiful half-dressed blond with a Russian accent. My eyes grow wide as she pulls her top down, baring her breasts to him and at first I see red, but then smile as I hear him tell her not to contact him again, but I can't get the picture of the handcuffs and the paddle out of my mind. That paddle, the one that is very similar if not the very one that I dreamed about Brian paddling me with, right there on the screen.

I can't take my eyes off of the scene in front of me. I know he's talking to me, but hardly hear what he's saying as I head back into the bedroom slamming the door behind me. I am barely controlling the rage that threatens to consume me looking at the beautiful woman that he's clearly had a relationship with. I look in the mirror trying hard not to compare myself to the voluptuous blonde. She knows his phone number and the things they did were obvious.

The door opens and he walks in closing it behind him. I am still looking in the floor length mirror. "Jenny, I haven't seen Sasha in over a month. We were together three times and I broke it off but she hasn't been easily persuaded," he says, running his hands through his jet black hair, his blue eyes watching me intently.

"You don't owe me any explanations about the relationship," I say, realizing that hearing he broke it off a month ago somewhat calms the jealous rage I'm feeling, but only somewhat.

"No, I don't but if the tables were reversed I would want to know," he says, coming to stand behind me, lifting my hair off my shoulders and kissing all the way down my neck. I moan softly, leaning into his tongue's caress.

"Did you use the handcuffs and that riding crop on her?" I ask, looking at him in the mirror.

His eyes capture mine and I see a look of hesitancy before he answers. "The handcuffs, yes. The riding crop no, but other implements. I have to admit when I saw it tonight all I could think about was the one you described in your dream. The one about me spanking your little pussy," he says, huskily.

"Would you do that to me someday?" I ask, as he pulls me into him and I feel his hardened length pushing against my ass.

"Do you want me to restrain you while I do it?" he asks.

"Yes," I say without hesitation.

"Beautiful," he says, turning me around to face him.

"Kneel, I want you to feel how hard I am for you, feel me pulsing in your mouth," he says as he loses his clothes, tossing them in a pile on the floor. I drop to my knees, tasting the tip, running my tongue around and in and out of his salty slit, allowing myself to savor it before wrapping his hard silkiness in my mouth and sliding down his length. I rub the area at his root, relishing in his manly groan, feeling the power of his throbbing cock and the fact that I'm causing him to feel this way.

"Enough," he says, pulling me up, guiding me to the over-stuffed armchair and easing me back into it. "Place your legs over each of the arms so that you're on display for me," he instructs, walking to his closet. He comes back with a paddle and while not exactly the same, it is close, it is silver handled and has a small rectangular paddle on it. I gasp as I see it and feel myself moistening in response.

"Spread your legs wider, I want to see all of your pussy. Do you know why you're being punished?"

I shake my head no.

"No sir is the appropriate response."

"No, sir," I reply.

"Slamming my doors not only once but twice along with a multitude of other transgressions. You know your safe words and I want you to use them if you need to. Raise your hands above your head," he says, walking behind the chair.

I feel the silkiness of his tie wrap around my wrists before he affixes it to something behind us. My chest is obscenely pushed out this way and I feel my own breathing pattern change and the wetness pooling in my center. He sits on the ottoman in front of me admiring his handy work, watching me. The normally crystalline light blue eyes are deep and smoky, glazed over with passion. You're absolutely glistening and I haven't even touched you, yet," he says, staring at the wetness between my legs, completely on exhibit to him in this position.

"We're going to start with ten, just like before. You'll count with me. I didn't restrain your legs, but expect you to keep them positioned as they are or we'll start over, understand?" he says.

I nod. "I need to hear you, Sweetheart," he says.

"I won't move my legs and if I do we start over," I repeat.

"Good girl," he says, running the tip of the implement over the swell of my breasts and across the erect tips of my nipples, down the flat cave of my belly, and lower, circling my mound with the rubber tip. He slides it along the crease, between my thighs and where my body connects, and then starts all over again, teasing my nipples with the soft rubber material before the crop comes down over the sensitive nub sending a shot of electricity straight to my center.

My hips push into the feel. "Your responsiveness could make for a very long and fun night. Stay still, Jenny," he says as the paddle unexpectedly comes down between my legs, right there, on the most sensitive spot imaginable and my pussy clenches tightly. "Count," he says.

"Two," I say, but only barely in time before the next one lands right in the same place and I hear myself mewling out the word three, as the next one lands again, "four," I say, but my body pushes into the wicked flicks of desire shooting through my center.

"Bad girls that slam my bedroom door in fits of tantrum receive punishments just like this. They get their pink little pussies paddled," he says and with that he spanks me lower, avoiding my clit, causing me to cry out with unreleased desire as he instead smacks the gentle underside of my ass not allowing me to come and holding me right on the brink.

The next three are rained down in slow succession leaving me panting as we hit ten. I squirm but he holds me still, placing his hand on my lower belly before gently licking my over-sensitized clit with his tongue, gently stroking it, causing me to moan and cry out, desperately trying not to remove my legs from the armchair, but frenzied with need.

He is in no hurry, teasing me, blowing on my heated core with this warm breath and then licking gently before nipping my clit with his teeth and sinking two fingers deep inside of me.

"You're fucking soaked for me Sweetheart," he says, finding that special little spot.

"Oh, right there," I cry out and he doesn't stop, in fact takes every breath I have as he pulls the longest orgasm from my body that I have ever had, leaving me shaking and trembling while he licks between the folds of the most sensitive spot on my body. He reaches up and unties the silky material, letting my arms down, rubbing my wrists before pulling me up and flipping us around so that I'm on top and able to watch as he pulls a condom on.

"I need to be buried to the hilt in your hot little pussy," he says as he guides me down and in one thrust I can feel him deep inside of me. I moan as he grasps my ass, guiding me up and down on top while he captures my nipples in his mouth, suckling them before nipping and sending jolts of electricity to my center. I feel myself begin to build again and it feels like hours, but it could have been moments. The pressure is rising and rising and I can feel myself clenching around him precariously at the edge.

"Come for me now," he instructs, pulling me down fast and hard on top of his throbbing cock. I let go, trembling around him as he continues to guide us through our release before allowing it to subside and me to crumble in his arms. He holds me closely for some time but then carries me to bed before heading into the bathroom to wash up. He returns with a warm cloth. "Open your legs for me Sweetheart," he says.

I open them tentatively never experiencing this type of intimacy with anyone. He's watching me intently and I let my legs fall to the sides.

He takes his time, gently washing my thighs and then my center, paying special attention to my folds. When he's done he kisses his way back up my body. "You are mine and I want you to let me take care of you in all ways," he says, curling me into his arms.

After a while we head into the kitchen and he hauls out a caramel cheesecake from the refrigerator while I pour a glass of wine. "Hmm, more sinful pleasures," I murmur as he dishes us each up a plate.

His eyes light up with mischief. "You're going to need the energy for later," he says and I can hear my own hitch of breath. He looks down at his phone and ignores it, but when it starts vibrating again he picks it up. "What?" he says seriously annoyed. "Okay, thanks for letting me know," he says, disconnecting.

What's the matter?" I ask as he disconnects.

"You want to fill me in on your visit to see Vicenti?" Brian asks, taking the bottle of wine from the counter and pouring himself a glass while refilling mine.

"You know Chase was arrested in a drug trafficking incident about a year ago?" I ask.

"Yep, I've heard parts of the story. I know Alfreita kidnapped Kate's mom to try and force Chase into using his shipping connections to smuggle drugs into the country and that Chase and Carlos teamed up, found her and got her back. I also know that Carlos Larussio is not going to stop until Alfreita is unable to harm his family," he says.

It's my turn to nod. "Chase got arrested for the trumped up drug trafficking charge and Kate took matters into her own hands at that point," I say with pride.

"So I've heard," Brian says wryly.

"She made Sheldon fly us to Brazil, needed help with PR and wanted a little moral support so asked me to go along. Jay gave her the info she needed to convince Vicenti that he had a dirty crew and that Alfreita and Tony were working to undermine his territory. Once she had Vicenti's backing everything fell into place. I don't know how it happened exactly, but the very next morning Chase was released."

TWENTY

BRIAN

"I don't doubt that Sweetheart. Vicenti has a massive sphere of control. I can't believe Jay's team let you and Kate go," I say, fuming at the incompetence.

"Umm, last time I checked Kate and I were of legal age. We would have gone with or without their consent," she says and my dick twitches at the heated look in her eyes.

"If I had known you then you and your sassy little mouth would have been put over my knee and you would have stayed home and out of danger," I say, hearing the catch in her breath.

"Too bad I didn't know you then," she says, flirting with me while she twirls her wine glass. She has no fucking clue how hot she is or how serious I am.

"I just wish everything with Alfreita would end. Kate said she thinks they're close but Chase won't give her any details," she says, sipping her wine.

"So what happened after you got to Brazil? All the newspaper said was charges had been lifted and Tony and Alfreita were implicated."

"We went to see Jay in the hospital. He gave us all the info on Vicenti," she says as though she's not talking about the man that runs the biggest cartel in South America.

"What the hell were they thinking letting you walk into a situation like that?"

"I guess you had to be there to appreciate the adventure. Can I have another glass of wine, or are you still limiting me?" she says sweetly, ignoring my outburst and twitch of my jaw.

"You always have choices, Sweetheart, but after you've finished the third and take the first sip of the fourth there's no turning back," I say, raising my glass in salute.

She smiles and her eyes flash. "Well in that case, cheers," she says, pouring a third.

"Cheers," I say, interested to see just how far she wants to push her limits.

"If you're worried someone recognized me, they couldn't. We were disguised when we went into the hospital and I didn't go with Kate to Vicenti's. You seriously should have seen Kate though, Brian. She was up all night practicing, rehearsing for the next day's conversation with Vicenti. She put on this outfit, short little black skirt, four-inch heels, button down blouse; suffice it to say that my best friend was looking the part of the hot little mafia daughter and billionaire's fiancée. It took a lot of guts to go into Vicenti's compound without a wire, but she did it. Let him hear the tape and the next day he and Sheldon had all the details worked out and Chase was a free man."

"Not exactly what I would consider free and Alfreita's still after his ass. I think you're taking the situation way too lightly," I say.

"Yeah, I think he struck out because Chase and Carlos cut off certain supplies making it almost impossible for him to make or move his product. They couldn't figure out who was financing him until Jay's team found out that leaders of Interpol were helping him."

I whistle. "Shit, it just keeps getting deeper and deeper," I say, wondering how the fuck they let her get involved in this mess.

"I'm sorry you ended up involved. I think Chase wanted to keep you protected, but then you had to bring me to your house," she says.

"You have nothing to be sorry for. Your dumbass security team on the other hand is on my shit list," I say, ignoring the flash in her eyes and twist of her lips as she takes the last sip of her third drink.

I am listening to this story and trying to absorb it all as she speaks. Not only do we have Alfreita to deal with, but I know from Scottie we have an uncle in Italy along with Dominic Mancini and now we have fucking Interpol connections at the highest levels of the organization.

I look up at her as she pours the fourth glass, gorgeous and oblivious to the danger. I haven't stopped her. As much as my threat is intended to curb her destructive habit, there's a part of me that is waiting, just watching and anxious to see if she'll take that sip. She knows I won't go easy on her and yet here she sits, swirling and inhaling the aroma of her fourth glass.

One sip, Sweetheart. As if she heard my thoughts she tips the crystal to her mouth. Her lips so close to the liquid I've forbidden is exciting to me and my dick twitches in acknowledgement. She's going to disobey me and I am going to punish her.

She swirls the liquid in her glass one more time, teasing me and I tip my head in challenge and response.

Her glass tilts and I give her one more warning with my eyes, but she takes the sip and then her pink tongue peeks out of her mouth and licks her lips, ensuring she tastes every bit of its sweetness. She goes to take another sip and before she can I put my hand on the glass heading back to those delectable little lips.

You're over your limit, Sweetheart," I say, putting her glass down, standing up and pulling her out of her seat and into my arms.

"It would appear that way," she says, taunting me with that sweet sassy mouth. My lips capture hers, while I caress the back of her neck, beneath the silkiness of her hair. She opens for me and I groan inwardly. I scoop her up and take her back into my bedroom and sit in the same armchair we were just in, contemplating her desire to be punished. She enjoys the pleasure that punishment provides and as much as that turns me on, I know in that instant how to truly punish her for the behavior I wish to correct.

I sit in the chair. "Undress slowly for me. I want to see all of your clothes off," I say.

She smiles at me. Damn it, she likes this so much and all I really want to do is turn her over my knee, spank her ass red and then bury my balls deep inside of her, but I also want her to take this seriously. I realize from Scottie's report that she hasn't been drinking heavily for so long that she can't control it. She can, and I'm going to make damn sure she does.

She's doing what I asked, slowly lowering her bra straps, the delicate lace holding her firm little tits in place. I watch mesmerized as she pulls the lace down, slowly exposing the swell of her breast, waiting with baited breath to see her nipple, but she leaves the material in place just enough to cover her little tips and begins the same routine on the other side.

My dick twitches in anticipation and I swallow down my desire and narrow my eyes at her. I am ready to explode by the time she lets the edge of the lace caress and expose her nipples and allows the material to hit the floor with her other clothes. Her hands are floating towards her hips and I look at her minis-cule lacy panties. I know exactly where she thinks this is going.

I take her hand and tug her across my knee, smiling at her gasp of surprise as I regain control. I run my hands over her beautifully round and firm ass cheeks. She is so small, but she is also feminine and the curves of her ass make me even harder. Her hands dangle in front of her and I steady her with a hand at her waist, placing my leg over the tops of her thighs. I hear her breath hitch at the constraint.

She knows her safe words and I have every confidence she'll use them if needed, but I also know she won't. She wants this. I could see it in the darkening of her eyes, the change of her breathing and the excitement of expectancy as she took that sip of wine. It's the anticipation of the unknown and that's what she'll learn more about tonight. I rub her ass gently with my hands and she does not anticipate the first slap. It comes down hard and fast as intended drawing a sharp intake of breath from her. It is immediately followed by two, three and four more. Her ass is getting warmer and I enjoy the pinkening of her skin as my hand spanks her again and again getting the response I intended. Now she is squirming, the warmth growing deep inside her little pussy as well as her ass. She grinds her little mound against me on the next down strike and it takes everything I have not to turn her over and pull her onto my rock hard cock as I finish with nine and ten. I run my hands over her ass, enjoying the warmth and she lays still not sure what to expect next which makes my cock twitch underneath her heated little pussy.

I pull her up and have her stand in front of me. Her face is flushed and her eyes are glossy with lust. Her breathing is shallow and I find it fascinating that her desire is so apparent, no games, she clearly knows what she wants even as new to this as she is, but she's only known pleasure up to this point and that's what she's expecting. She's anticipating that I will make her come. While I'd like nothing better than to see her moaning and mewling beneath me, I will have to get by with hearing her begging tonight.

I grasp her hips and my hands slide over her ass, down to her gently curving thighs, pushing them outward slightly so her legs widen for me. Her pussy is now on display for me and I part her lips so that I can see her glistening wetness. It is an aphrodisiac and I lean in and inhale her special scent, all mine and the need to mark her is strong but I push it down, knowing that tonight she needs to know who is in control. I will always do whatever it takes to keep her safe and that means from her own foolishness as well as danger from others. I blow on her clit and I can see the slight quiver of her thigh before I touch her mound with my tongue.

She tilts her hips and I steady her. "If you move again we start over," I say, opening her and blowing on her pulsing clit. I touch her with my tongue and my cock throbs hard when she purrs. I lick her again, the creamy sweetness causing me to rethink my own intentions and it is with barely a thread of control that I bring myself back into the moment, the intent, moving my tongue slightly, right off the mark, teasing her. She knows not to squirm, but I can tell she wants to. Her hands go to my hair.

Naughty girl! I smile, knowing she needs to be restrained. I guide her to the bed and lay her down, crawling on top of her. I kiss the softness of her neck and capture her skin as I knot the silky ties around her wrists. I watch intently to see if it gets a response from her of fear or anxiety, but she is lusty and ready, eyes full of desire and anticipation.

"Now that you're restrained feel free to move all you want," I say as I work my way down her body, licking her collarbone, suckling her neck and it is with great restraint that I keep myself from marking her, traveling over the swell over her breasts, taking in her nipples, suckling them and then sucking hard, just the way she likes it. She moans aloud and writhes underneath me making it difficult to concentrate. I finally get to her navel, that tiny sensitive little area. I lick it gently, rewarded with the upward motion of her hips. I make my way south and push her legs apart, gently opening her wider for my enjoyment and to watch that lovely blush shine onto her cheeks. She is absolutely soaked, I lick her gently and she mewls against me and moans. I know she's close already and I'm careful to bring her up slowly, keeping her hot, writhing on the end of my tongue which keeps caressing her, on and then just off the mark. Her hips are moving on their own accord and her breathing has become erratic and I slowly make my way back up her body, lingering to enjoy her before I gently kiss her beautiful pouty lips. "I think now it's time for your punishment to begin," I say.

"Brian?" she says and the look she gives me almost does me in. What I want to do is take my cock out and come all over her beautiful little pouty lips, show her that for taking the sip of wine she's going to lay here aching all night while I come all over her mouth, but it might be too cruel for her first punishment.

"Time for you to lay here all night with your pussy wet and throbbing," I say, leaving her tied up and panting while I head into the bathroom and run a shower for myself. She won't push this limit again after tonight.

Just the thought of her laying there wet and ready for me, so needy has me sliding my hand over the rigid shaft of my cock and in a mere matter of minutes I'm releasing all the pent up desire that woman has caused. I shower letting her lay there aching for a while longer before I return to the bedroom.

She has somehow managed to flip over and her little round ass is on display for me and her hands are outstretched in my bed. Fuck, this might end up backfiring as I look at that sweet little ass that I was spanking not an hour ago. I briefly think about fucking her in that position but her breathing is soft and controlled and she is fast asleep. I untie her and damn if she doesn't turn into my chest and find my heartbeat. I pull the sheet over the top of us and flip over trying to keep the image of her ass in the air out of my mind, but fuck my dick is hard again just thinking about her laying there with a hot little pussy.

TWENTY-ONE

JENNY

I am so close and so wet that I can feel it on my inner thighs. I don't think I have ever been this turned on. All the fantasies I've ever had, dreamed about, masturbated to, were nothing compared to what he's done to me and now I'm tied up and lying here soaking wet listening to him shower. Just the thought of his lean sculpted body, broad shoulders, tapered waist, rock hard abs and powerful thighs and ass letting the water flow over them makes my pussy clench with unleashed desire.

I manage to flip over. Why would he do this? Most men would have shoved their cock inside of me and had their way, but he doesn't want me to drink more than I should, so he punishes me to keep me protected? Somehow that calms me; the thought that this man cares enough to deny me in order to make his point instead of selfishly taking what he needs calms me and that is the last thing I can think about as I fall into a peaceful sleep.

When I wake, Brian's side of the bed is empty, but my hands have been untied sometime in the night. I glance over at his pillow and there is a note lying on top of it.

D o not touch yourself Sweetheart. I will know.

I smile as I get out of bed and head for the shower, quickly washing, getting ready for the day. He's in the kitchen in his lounge pants with no shirt or shoes. I can feel the heat on my cheeks just watching him. He looks up with a smirk on his face as I glance at him. "Hungry gorgeous?" he asks.

"I'm absolutely ravenous, like I've been thoroughly deprived of a delicious meal all night," I say, looking into his crystalline blue eyes and finding them alight with amusement.

He pours me a cup of coffee out of the carafe and adds a little creamer. "Good, then I assume three drinks will be your limit going forward," he says.

"Uh-huh," I say, inhaling and intentionally ignoring him. "I know the K-Cups are all the rage, but I love the experience of grinding my own beans and then letting them brew. Just the smells alone are enough to get your senses going in the morning, and then add a little creamy sweet caramel, and oh my God," I say, licking my bottom lip.

He narrows his eyes at me and his mouth upturns in a quirk. He doesn't rise to my bait but Celia smirks as she walks in and I feel my cheeks reddening realizing she's overheard our exchange before she gives me a grin and a wink, leaving a platter with spinach quiche and fruit before discreetly disappearing.

"This looks amazing," I say, dishing both of us a piece along with a large helping of the cut up papaya, mango, and cantaloupe. "I wonder if it tastes as good as it looks," I say, selecting a slice of mango and licking the tip before sliding and sucking the length into my mouth.

His eyes darken and he looks like he is about to say something when his phone rings. "Damn it, excuse me for a sec," he says, answering the device but never taking his eyes off of me.

"Brian here, any word?" he says, pausing to let the caller speak. His jaw tightens and he runs his hand through his hair. "Not good enough. I know they're just sending a message, but damn it Chase, I need to know what the plan is. Get this handled so we can get the fuck out of this condo," Brian says.

He listens for a while and nods. "Keep me posted and I'll try to keep Scottie and his men on this side of civil," he says, disconnecting. His phone begins vibrating again and he immediately connects, listening for a while as he intermittently takes bites of his breakfast.

"Thanks for the update, Scottie, keep me posted," he says, hanging up after quite some time and looking utterly annoyed.

"Brian, what's going on? I say.

"Carlos went to Brazil earlier today and all hell is breaking loose right now."

"Did he go see Vicenti? I ask.

"Yes, and Carlos is putting his life on the line talking to Vicenti when his uncle knows that he wants to sell the family business to him and is dead set against it."

"Then why wouldn't Carlos just sell to his uncle?" I ask, shaking my head in confusion.

"It's complicated. Carlos has been working on going completely legit for years and the only thing in his way is his uncle and Alfreita. You know the information he sent you about the Vegas acquisitions?"

"In all honesty, I barely skimmed through them but I know that Carlos is going to be one of the largest land owners on the strip shortly. I asked Kate if she would take over Torzial for a little bit. Dr. Werther suggested that I take a few weeks off of work to focus on healing," I say.

He nods. "That makes sense. Kate's got a good head on her shoulders for business. Hopefully she'll have enough time to maintain Torzial, too," he says.

"It's only supposed to be for a couple weeks."

"Okay, I'm just looking out for you," he says.

"If you are looking out for my well-being and going a little stir crazy in this huge penthouse you might try fucking me," I counter.

He stalks right over to me and picks me up, capturing my lips, crushing me against him and carries me straight into his bedroom. He lets me slide down his body and I feel his hardened length push against me as he lets my feet slowly touch the ground.

"Strip for me," he instructs.

Everything south clenches at his command and I do it without hesitation. My clothes are in a small pile on the floor and in a matter of seconds I am bare and quivering with anticipation. He pushes me onto the bed and spreads my thighs until each of them are resting against the mattress. "Hold that pose, Sweetheart," he says, wrapping my wrists in the silky material of his tie that was lying on the bed. He places my bound hands over head and attaches them to the headboard. He then opens the nightstand drawer and takes out a black mask and positions it over my eyes. "Don't move and remember your safe words," he says and I hear the bedroom door open and close.

I sigh heavily. I thought my punishment had ended and it's clear that he's going to continue making me wait. My body is pent-up with unreleased desire and I would give anything to be able to free my hands and place my finger between my own legs. I am briefly contemplating the ways I could flip and cause some much needed friction when the door opens and recloses.

"Good girl, you didn't move. Spread open for me just the way

I left you," he says and a second later his finger is tracing the length from my knee to my inner thigh circling a pattern there. I'm holding my breath desperately wanting him to touch me there and my breath hitches as his finger finally moves toward my center.

"Do you trust me to pleasure you, Jenny?" he asks.

I nod. "I need words, I need to hear you say it and that you remember your safe word," he says.

"I trust you, Brian and I'll use my safe word if I need to," I say and at that very moment I feel warmth drizzled on the calf of my right leg and along my thigh before the hot liquid is dripping onto the top of my mound. I am focused on the pooling liquid that is spilling around my center when he begins with the other calf, swirling the warmth over my inner thighs before trickling more onto my mound. I inhale deeply, trying hard not to move my legs but I desperately want to feel the warmth on my clit and he's drizzling it everywhere except for there. He gently takes my unbound ankle and moves it out to the side and swirls his tongue along my calf and begins tracing the same pattern up to my inner thigh. When he gets to my center he blows on my clit and I moan aloud.

"Shh, Sweetheart," he says and I clench my hands unable to grip into the sheets or anything else while he continues to tease my oversensitive body. He is in no hurry and does the same with my other leg. Gently placing my ankle outward while licking and suckling the tender skin all the way up the inside of my legs.

"This is exactly how I like my dessert served Jenny. I enjoy it open, the scent of arousal strong and I especially like when I can see the creamy little middle pooling with my eyes," he says and I can feel the heat of my cheeks flushing as he kisses the top of my mound.

"Do you know how I like to eat my dessert?" he asks.

I shake my head side to side, barely able to control my breathing. I desperately need him to touch me there and I know he can see my inner muscles clenching with unreleased desire.

"No, sir," he says, blowing on my clit.

I gasp at the sensation. "No, sir," I say without hesitation.

"I like lots and lots of sweet warm gooey caramel covering it," he says at the same time he begins drizzling thick warm liquid all over my clit. I moan at the feel and my hips rise of their own accord and then I feel his tongue. "Brian," I cry out as his tongue flicks over my clit once but then concentrates on licking the caramel from my folds, avoiding it again.

"Now, when I ask you if three drinks will be your limit, how will you respond next time," he asks.

"Yes, sir," I say, desperate to feel his tongue.

"Good girl," he says, washing my clit with the velvety warm wetness of his tongue, causing me to grind against him. He licks me gently over and over, bringing me to the edge and then holding, making me squirm relentlessly below him before he sucks hard and the climax that has been right on the brink plummets in wave after wave as I come, causing me to cry out.

"That's right Sweetheart, let me hear you. I've been waiting for this since last night and I want my dessert, that creamy delicious filling," he says, pushing my legs farther apart, running his tongue down my seam before dipping it into my center.

"Brian, it's too much. I'm too sensitive," I moan, but he doesn't stop and after a few moments my body relaxes and begins to savor the deliciously slow build up again.

"I want to see your eyes when I'm fucking you," he says, pushing my knees to my chest, settling in between my legs so that he can push the blindfold off my eyes. He's already protected and is holding his cock in his hand. "I want to fuck you hard and fast but tell me if it's too much," he says, pushing in with one thrust. In this position, I can feel him deep in my center and I moan as he hits that special spot and he does it over and over again until I am panting and crying out his name as he brings us both over the edge and we are trembling in the aftermath.

TWENTY-TWO

BRIAN

We are **curled up sated** from our lovemaking and still lying in bed when my phone rings. I listen and then disconnect the call. "That was Chase. There's been a lot of activity and Alfreita's men have moved out of the city. It doesn't mean that there isn't risk, but the level of security has been decreased," I say to Jenny.

"That's great. So Matt and I won't be cooped up in the condo any longer?" she asks.

I cringe inwardly. I know she hates being kept inside even though the penthouse is ten times larger than her apartment. "I'm not comfortable with that. Matt will continue to be your point, but you'll now have a team of security and they will report directly to him," I say.

She narrows her eyes at me. "You know I appreciate everything you've done, but I'm fine with Matt. He's been taking care of me for quite some time now," she says.

I don't respond. I hate that she wants him with her all the time. I've seen the way he looks at her and she doesn't even notice. He wants her for his own. I've scoured the surveillance tapes that Scottie was able to get from Jay. I have to give him credit. He has never once crossed a line, never once shown anything that can be construed as anything but business, but I see the look in his eyes when he's watching her. The fact that she wants to go back to her own condo with Matt pisses me right the fuck off, it creates this need within me to hit something. I know he would die before he let anything happen to her and that's why he's been put in charge of her but right now he should steer the fuck clear of me.

"Brian."

"What, Sweetheart," I say, pulling her close.

"I need to go back to my apartment and deal with trying to go to sleep on my own knowing he's out there. If I am ever going to get back to myself, I have to get past the fear of being alone. It scares the hell out of me, but if I don't do this I'm scared I'll never get me back."

I contemplate this for a few moments. She's not ever going to be on her own but her confidence has been taken and she needs to get this back. I don't tell her that there's no way in fuck that she'll ever be without my security team watching over her.

"Whatever you need, Sweetheart," I say.

"I really appreciate that you have been there for me, sheltered me, kept me safe but if I am ever going to move on I need to do this," she says.

Her courage is bold and unique and I know looking into her deep green depths that this is something she has to do. I nod, knowing I have an entire army of security around her and that she will be physically safe but the one that wants her will be with her and I won't. I fucking hate that!

How is it that this woman has managed to get under my skin to such a degree? I kiss her and get out of bed and go out to the kitchen while she gets ready for the day. I throw a K-Cup in the machine and begin going over the structure for Carrington Steel. I look up when she walks into the kitchen freshly showered and dressed for the day in a short skirt and ankle boots. She puts a coffee pod in for herself before she joins me at the table.

"Still working on your structure?" she asks, glancing at my computer and the algorithm in front of me.

"Yeah, I think it's a wrap. I'm just putting the communication plan together and working with the human resources department to get all the details aligned," I say.

"If you need a project plan template, Kate and I put one together for all the Torzial expansion work and she's got a ton for the work on the Prestian Corp facilities. You can just have your associates modify the details," she says.

"I might just take you up on that," I say, closing my laptop.

She gets up to retrieve her coffee from the machine and I can't take my eyes off of her. She turns and her eyes meet mine.

"What's the matter," she says.

"I'm going to have you stay here for a few more days, possibly another week while we get your condo ready and decide what the next steps are," I hear myself saying.

"You're going to have me stay here?" she asks, narrowing her eyes at me.

"Yes, and if you argue with me I'm going to bend you over and spank your ass until you can't sit down for a week and then I'm going to fuck you until you can barely walk," I say.

I hear the hitch in her breathing and the pattern change. "Brian, I know you want me to stay for another week and I sincerely thought about it, but I think I should go back today. I can't let what he's done leave me shattered. I need to take back control and be free of him once and for all."

She's being open and honest with me about her needs and she believes that she has to take this step so I concede. "Whatever you need, Sweetheart," I say.

"I need to get some groceries in the house and try to get a routine down. I'm going to give myself a little bit of time before I go back to work. Kate's got everything under control and I might even take a self-defense class. My counselor talked to me about it when we visited. I just need to do something to feel a little bit more in control of what happens to me. Well, outside of our relationship," she says shyly.

I smirk, knowing how much she likes me to take control in the bedroom and nod. "That sounds completely reasonable. If you'd like I can have Scottie look around for the best classes although I have to say you did a pretty amazing job without official training. Christ, you broke his nose and drove it right into his sinus cavity."

"Yeah, but maybe with training I could have prevented the asshole from getting me in that position to begin with. I was so scared when I heard his voice that I literally froze. If Scottie can locate a place for self-defense classes I would be grateful. I might even be able to get Kate to take it with me," I say.

"I'll have a driver give you and Matt a ride home, but you'll have more security than just him. Alfreita and Interpol seem to be out of the picture, but I'm not convinced that it's over, yet," Brian says.

"Okay, I'm going to pack and be on my way then," she says, and turns quickly heading back into the bedroom.

I don't know what the fuck I thought. I was just going to keep her here forever? What the fuck is wrong with me? Hit 'em and quit 'em, and I shake my head because the reality is that I want nothing more than to go and grab her, kiss her until she can barely breathe, and take her back to my bedroom and keep her there indefinitely. Indefinitely. Definitely more than a day, a week, a month, in-fucking-definitely.

She comes back into the kitchen packed and has made her decision. I pull her close and love the feel of her arms entwined around my neck. I want her as my own, but in what sense? I need to take time to figure this out while she's gaining her independence.

"Thanks for helping me get me back," she says, kissing me.

"Text me when you're all settled in," I say, giving her another light kiss on the lips.

She has most of her stuff in a small overnight bag and I will myself to let her walk out, trying my hardest to focus on what she needs and not what I so desperately want. I send a text to Scottie.

Message: No one lets her out of their fucking sight!

Reply: No lad, we've got every angle under surveillance.

I do not reply but instead put the best scotch that money can buy into a glass and bring it to my lips. I pause for a moment, wondering if that may be how she felt as she worked through all the demons in her life.

TWENTY-THREE

JENNY

att and I walk into my condo and look around. "The entire apartment has been swept," he says, holding the door for me.

"Thanks, Matt. I don't know what I'd do without you," I say, looking around. The apartment smells fresh; a lemony scent fills my nostrils as we get closer to the kitchen.

"Brian asked me to have the place cleaned before you returned. Kate gave me Sara's number," he says.

I look around and there are fresh flowers in a vase on the dining room table, an assortment of pink and yellow, with cherry red berries intermingled in a clear crystal vase. I head toward my bedroom and my body literally freezes. The last time I was here Brian had to carry me out after beating Ty to a pulp. I try to get a handle on my breathing, which has become erratic, and I force myself to keep moving in order to walk through that door. The room has been completely cleaned. The bed is made and none of the blood that was everywhere is left. Even the comforter is different. I look up at Matt who is watching me intently. "Brian?" I ask.

"He had a company come in after you guys left, but Kate picked out the bedspread and a few other details in the room."

"Because the sheets and the comforter were covered in blood," I say, not looking for an answer in particular but he nods.

I hug myself around the middle, cold, although the temperature in the condo is comfortable. I walk out of the bedroom trying to get his image out of my head and open the refrigerator. Not much in the way of food in there. "I think I'm going to busy myself with a little recipe planning. Are you staying here?" I ask Matt.

"I'll be wherever you want me to be," he says.

"I need to fight this feeling of being alone. I need to figure out how to drive the fear down and sleep without alcohol, and without you guarding me from my couch eventually," I say.

"I won't pretend to know what you went through and how terrifying it was, but you tell me what you need and that's what's going to happen," he says.

"I think for right now I'm going to have a little recipe therapy. Can I let you know about logistics, later?" I ask, pulling my magnetic notepad off the refrigerator, opening my laptop and googling a recipe site.

"Of course," he says, heading toward the reading chair in the corner of the living room where he can continue to observe me.

I sift through online recipes and after a couple of hours have menus for the next week. "I'm heading to the grocery store," I say once I have my list compiled.

"Brian has a driver on standby to take us and security is all set," he says.

"Matt, I'm trying to get back into the real world," I scold.

"Brian's right to have additional security. There's still risk out there."

"Fine," I say, grabbing my purse and heading toward the door.

"We need to wait for the driver. It shouldn't be more than a few moments," he says.

"I was going to drive myself, you know, like get in my own vehicle and steer my car to the grocery store," I say.

"That's not going to happen right now."

I get into the back of the limo irritated and text Brian a message.

Message: The goal was to become self-sufficient again.

Reply: And you will, eventually.

Message: Today, not tomorrow! Why are you purposely making me wait?

Reply: I happen to know it makes your pussy wet.

Message: Not outside the bedroom… it pisses me off.

Reply: If need be, we can have this discussion in the bedroom.

I decide not to reply and take my time at the grocery, skimming the contents from aisle to aisle. There's absolutely nothing that I have to do, no rush. It's actually a surprisingly enjoyable experience, one that's usually a hurried dash to pick up necessities. Matt keeps a fair amount of distance and is even a good sport about stopping by a local seasoning shop.

The afternoon flies by as I focus on normal things like putting groceries away, and rearranging the pantry and cabinets. I settle on preparing a lemon and kale salad with seared salmon for dinner. When I take Matt a plate he's watching television and eyes it warily. "Thanks, are you experimenting?" he asks, looking at the plate filled with greens as I take a seat across from him on the love seat.

I laugh. "Come on! It has parmesan cheese, bread crumbs, and the dressing is made with olive oil, lemon juice, and garlic. It sounded delicious when I was looking through recipes," I say, curling my feet underneath me and taking a bite.

"It did, huh? I suppose you didn't come across lasagna and garlic bread or anything like that for this coming week," he says before taking a huge forkful of salad.

"Sorry, not on the list, but I can easily make some for you," I say, laughing as he places the leafy greens in his mouth.

"Actually this salad isn't half bad," he says after chewing a few bites.

"Well, I'm certainly glad you approve. Try the salmon, it's not too bad if I do say so myself."

"Now that's really good and I'm usually not even a fish guy.

Have you given any thought to arrangements for tonight?" he asks.

"Yeah, would you mind hanging out at least for a few nights? I just don't think I'm quite ready to be alone," I say.

"Not a problem. Brian had the entire condo relocked and a new high-tech security system put into place so that should make you feel a lot more secure, but I'll stay as long as you need me to."

I narrow my eyes at him. "When did he do that?"

"I take it he didn't mention it to you," he says, finishing his dinner and standing up to take both of our plates into the kitchen.

"I had no idea. He must have worked it out with the land-lord," I say.

"He really didn't tell you anything, huh?" Matt says, shaking his head and trying to contain his amusement.

"Nope, appears I'm missing out."

"The landlord didn't want the security system that Jay and Scottie settled on so Brian now owns the building."

"Un-fucking-believable! He's seriously worse than Chase," I say, shaking my head and getting up to pour a glass of wine. I start the coffee pot with decaffeinated coffee, knowing that's the only thing Matt will drink tonight and then start loading the dishes into the washer.

"Yeah, it's a pretty close toss-up. He wasn't even fully happy about the system they had to go with but older wiring in this building wasn't compatible with the one he wanted. He's seriously had me giving him an update just about every hour in addition to the ones I send through to Jay and Scottie. The guy's pretty hands on, that's for sure," he says.

I smile. That's an understatement if I've ever heard one. "I'm heading to bed for the evening. Thanks for staying," I say.

"I'll be here if you need anything," he says, flipping open his laptop.

The room is the same as it was earlier and my pulse begins racing again stepping into it. I walk to the window checking that it's locked but I know that's not how Ty got in. He was given a key, by people who were paid to keep the building safe, but fell for his bullshit story. I feel bad the guy lost his job but feel safer knowing the entire staff have been retrained. I still can't believe Brian bought the entire building and had a new security system put in place.

I head into the shower and think about the last time Brian and I showered together. The way the water cascaded over his chest, lean cut abs, over his throbbing cock and it's all I can do to finish washing without touching myself.

I towel off, blow dry my hair until it's silky smooth, slide into bed, and try to read for a bit but it's impossible. My mind keeps replaying the last time with Brian, the way he took me, so hard and feral. I look around the room and shiver. I need another fucking drink to obliterate the things that have gone on in this room right the hell out of my mind.

I slide on a robe and head into the kitchen. Matt looks up but two drinks is nothing when he's used to me drinking so much more. I pour another glass of wine and then lock my door and slip off my robe, cozying back into bed, leaning against the headboard. I pull the satiny sheets up to cover me as I sip my wine and browse the apps on my iPad. I hover over FaceTime for a few moments and finally hit the button to connect to Brian.

He's sitting at the kitchen table with his laptop and I see a glass of scotch next to him.

"Hi there, just wanted to tell you thank you for everything that you did. Matt told me you bought the complex and had an electronic security system put in place," I say.

"You're welcome. Is that all you wanted to tell me?" he asks, taking a sip of his scotch.

"Well, I'm halfway through my second glass of wine so I might have more to share later?"

"The three drink rule still applies," he says.

"It was easy not to drink with you around. Tonight may be a bit of a challenge," I say.

"What do you need, Sweetheart?"

"I feel safe when you're in control. I'm struggling with being by myself tonight," I say.

"What happened to needing to be alone?" he asks.

"It's overrated," I say, taking a sip of my wine.

"Put your glass down. Lay it on the nightstand next to you," he says.

I do it immediately. "Is your door locked?" he asks.

"Yes."

"Go unlock it, I want you to think about someone coming into your room and catching you being a naughty girl."

I do as he asks without question. "Now completely undress and turn the camera for me. Let me see your perky little tits and lay back on the bed so I can see all of you," he says.

My core clenches listening to him and I do what he says.

"Your nipples are so hard. Squeeze them for me, just the way I would," he says and I do, pinching them, barely containing a moan as I feel it in my center and watch his crystalline blue eyes darken.

"Don't stop, keep rubbing them between your fingers and thumb, pretend it's me making you moan and creating that moistness between your legs. Let me hear how you like it, Sweetheart," he says.

I moan.

"Now rub your little pussy for me," he says.

I moan again, rising into my hands, letting my finger slide over my folds and the little nub that is screaming for pleasure, gently at first but the heat is too much and I begin to raise my hips.

"You're too close. Stop rubbing your clit and focus on your nipples. Both of your fingers and thumbs, take them and squeeze, hard, like I would do and then begin to leisurely roll them," he instructs.

I look into his eyes and do as he commands, whimpering as my climax dissipates. The waves start to rebuild as I squeeze my nipples and I feel myself clenching with unleashed desire. "God,

Brian, I wish you were here fucking me, that's what I need," I say, moaning.

"Push the sheets down with your French tipped little toes; let me see you slide it away from your skin, all the way down."

I do, my toes curling to grasp the sides of the sheets. "Push them down farther Sweetheart, let me see your bare little mound and let me see you rub yourself," he says as I slide the satiny sheet down my body.

"Can you see?" I ask hoarsely.

"Oh, Sweetheart, I can see how fucking wet you are for me. Stop touching yourself, right now. Put the speaker on and lay the iPad on the bed," he instructs.

"Okay, but it feels so good," I moan, still slowly running my finger through that special spot.

"If you come I'll punish you."

"Oh, God, what if I can't stop?

"Then I'll spank your little ass until its red and you can't sit down for a week."

"Tell me what you want me to do," I say.

"Move your fingers; run them up and onto your navel. Let them caress that little space, but not too fast, slow, let them feel like I'm just caressing, licking your little button very slow, touch it like I do," he says.

"Oh, God, Brian," I say, my body rising up to meet my fingers.

"You're almost all the way gone. Slow down now, slide your finger in and out of your pussy. I want to see it glistening."

I moan out loud struggling for control. "You feel that Sweet-heart?" he says as my hips rise on their own accord.

"Now you're going to feel the air change, a breeze over your clit, then my finger touching you, feeling how wet you are for me and then you're going to feel my tongue on your little clit," he says as I start when I hear the door handle begin to turn.

"Don't stop on my account Sweetheart," he says, walking into the bedroom, laying his cell phone down and pulling his tie off in two quick strokes. The moon and city lights are streaming into the room providing me with a view of his shirt coming off, his gleaming torso and rock hard abs as he undresses himself. He is standing over me and rubs my slit with his finger. "So wet for me, Sweetheart," he says before lowering himself to run his tongue over my clit, causing me to shiver with unleashed desire.

He teases me for what seems an eternity before suckling my clit, causing me to tremble and shake against him as he continues to suck me through my pleasure. He pushes my legs over my head and buries his cock into me until he's so deep, and I am so full. My hips rise to meet him, thrust for thrust, my desire rebuilding as he repositions my legs and sinks deeper causing me to audibly moan, hitting that special little spot over and over before we finally find our release together and he curls me into his warmth.

"Stay with me tonight, Brian," I say, finding that place on his chest where I can listen to his beating heart. I have barely taken a few breaths before I am overcome with emotion and exhaustion and fall asleep.

TWENTY-FOUR

BRIAN

As soon as I hit the accept button and see those green depths staring at me, wide and unsure, I regret letting her go. I don't know how I've gone from not wanting to spend a night even sleeping with a woman to not wanting to spend one night without her in my arms.

I've thought about her all day making Matt give me updates every hour. I saw red when he messaged me that he was taking her shopping. He's her security, paid to protect her, but damn if it didn't make my blood boil. And when I read the text that they just finished a meal she made and was trying out on him, he almost lost his job. It took every ounce of willpower not to have Chase remove him from her detail. It was only after receiving the update that she had gone to bed with a glass of wine for the night that I settled down enough to focus on getting even a little work done. As soon as she called that plan was shot to hell.

The text to my driver was short, letting him know I would be downstairs in less than five minutes. "Where to boss?" Wes says as I slide into the backseat of the limo.

"Jenny's," I say before hitting the privacy glass.

Alerted to my impending arrival Matt answers the door. "She's in the room straight ahead to the right." I fucking loved the way she looked when I walked through the door. Legs spread open so I could watch her fingers stroking herself and those glazed over lustful looking eyes.

I look down now at her sleeping body and push the long wavy hair that's fallen over her face out of her eyes. I know she feels completely safe with me and I kiss her gently on the forehead before settling in for the night. I've gone from not allowing anyone even at my house or bed, to following her to her bed and staying the night.

When I wake she is watching me, her eyes wide and intent.

"Morning," she says, smiling.

That smile, all for me, and then she licks her bottom lip. Fuck me, my hard-on is already raging and I crush her lips to me. She lets out a little purr and my dick expands. I know it's juvenile, but I want to mark her, want her to know and see that she belongs to me and only me. I want everyone to know she belongs to me when she's out and about and not with me. She writhes into me as I suckle her neck, nipping her before dipping into that sensitive little spot between her neck and collarbone. She moans softly and I rub her little pussy, finding it already wet and ready for me.

In one swift move I'm wrapped and my cock needs no help finding its way into her velvety warmth. When we are finally sated and our breathing returns to normal, I carry her to the shower, washing her body and hair. I don't know what the hell is wrong with me. I don't fucking do romance but the desire for possession and intimacy with this woman is almost primal.

I dress quickly while she's blow drying her hair, settling into the arm chair adjacent to the window. I look at the tell-tale signs of security around the windows and grimace. It's substandard but much better than what was previously in place, but there's no safe room and as much as I thought I could deal with her moving back in before it's completely renovated, it's un-fuck-ing-acceptable to me.

She walks into the bedroom and my eyes drink her in, the short skirt, black heeled boots and a little sweater thing that covers her shoulders and lays enticingly over the swell of her chest. She sees me looking and her cheeks pinken. "I'm starving, I'll make some breakfast for the three of us while you finish with whatever you're doing," she says.

The three of us? Not likely Sweetheart. "Maybe another time. Celia will have breakfast prepared shortly. Pack enough clothes for a few days and I'll have someone come back for the rest," I find myself saying.

She looks at me as though I've lost my mind and I think I have. She's not staying here with him, these thin walls and this lackluster attempt at security. "I just got back, you put security in place, you bought the entire building," she says.

"Yes, and it's going to take a lot longer to bring this place up to the standards that either Scottie or Jay require, and let's not forget the thin walls. There's no way I could possibly spank you the way I want here," I say, going back to the work on my laptop.

I can feel her eyes on me, penetrating me like they do. "I'm going to go make breakfast," she says and begins to walk past me.

I pull her into my lap. I know what she wants damn it, I see it in her eyes and I immediately feel remorse. "Alright, I'm a total ass. I want you to come home with me because I want to keep you safe, want to protect you, and I can't think about anything but you when you're not with me," I say, wiping a little tear that has pooled in the corner of her eyes. "I'm also a very possessive man. I don't want you to spend one more day under the same roof with Matt without me."

She opens her mouth and I capture her lips to silence her. "You are mine and I don't fucking share," I say, pressing into her.

She opens to me and snakes her hands around my neck bringing me to her. "I just wanted to hear that you care," she says, nuzzling herself into me.

"I fucking care, Sweetheart," I say, holding her close and wondering how I'll even let her out of my sight again.

I text Scottie to let him know the plans and it's not long before I get a smart ass text back from him. I smirk and don't respond. He's one of the few I'll take this shit from. The car pulls around to pick us up and Wes navigates the congested Chicago city traffic and Matt and security are driving in front of and behind us.

The elevator opens into the penthouse and the smell of fresh pineapple, maple syrup, and waffles waft through the air. "This looks wonderful, I'm absolutely starving," Jenny says as we take our seats at the table and I give Celia a wink of thanks for getting everything prepared so quickly.

We're almost finished with brunch when my cell vibrates. "Excuse me a moment," I say, frowning.

"Brian, Chase here. Carlos got in safe from Brazil last night. The time he spent with Vicenti went well. The plans for the Vegas properties should proceed as planned, but he's still dealing with his brothers and uncle. Jay and I are on our way to work through a situation with Alfreita and won't be back until tomorrow night. I was going to ask you if you could have Jenny stay at your house or at our place to be with Katarina, but Jay tells me you moved her back in."

"That's affirmative, she's here with me."

"Sheldon's on point with Katarina until my return, but if things go south could you take care of a few things for me?"

"Anything you need, Chase," I say.

"I'll send you a secure zip through the Prestian portal. It has specific instructions and documents in the event something happens. My attorney has access as well. Jay said he has Matt on point with Jenny. Is he with you?" he asks.

"Yes, he's staying downstairs in the safe room where he can

monitor the perimeter, communication between the security staff, and has a clear visual of all entry points," I say.

"Greatly appreciate you taking care of things in my absence, Brian," Chase says.

"It's not a problem. Keep in touch and good luck," I say, before disconnecting.

It is later in the evening when Jenny's cell phone rings. "Kate, how are you? I was wondering when I would receive my next call," she says, jokingly.

"Oh my God! Kate, Brian's here and I'm putting you on speakerphone. Kate's parents were in a car accident," she mouths to me and then asks Kate, "When are you going?"

"We're on our way now. We just boarded the jet and are leaving for the trauma center in a few moments," Kate says.

"Kate, this is Brian. I'm real sorry to hear about your parents. Sheldon is your security point, correct?" he asks.

"Yes, he's been great. He contacted the hospital and the police department to confirm the accident and has security blanketing the perimeter of the hospital," she says.

"I know that you aren't able to contact Chase right now and I want to make sure you're okay while he's gone. You don't fucking trust anyone, and do not go anywhere on your own. I know it's hard to think about while your concern is for your parents, but you need to understand that Alfreita's team may know you're out of the complex," Brian says.

"I understand. I called Chase's dad and he told me the same

thing and talked to Sheldon, too. I really appreciate you both looking out for me," she says.

"Call or text when you arrive. I'll connect with Sheldon and sincerely hope all is well with your parents when you arrive," I say before disconnecting and placing a call to Sheldon.

"Brian here, Kate tells me you've confirmed the accident and the trauma. How did she find out?" I ask as Jenny watches me intently.

"Police officer contacted her so I needed to make sure it was legit. I should have heard about this from Carlos's head of security, but the son of a bitch is either pissed off that we're involved or dirty. I've got our men looking into things and intel starting to go through communication exchanges in and out of their complex in the last few weeks," Sheldon says.

"Excellent. I'll let Scottie know that you may need more assistance while Jay and Chase are gone. Keep me posted and let me know when you land," I say, before disconnecting.

I hit Scottie's phone number and he answers immediately.

"Carlos Larussio and his wife Karissa were in an accident. Check into it, no details yet from this end except that it's bad and they were being rushed to the trauma center. I need you to get eyes on the security head for Carlos. Sheldon's getting a bad vibe, no communication on this at all to the internal team or the person taking care of his daughter. Send in one of our own teams to meet them at the airport, escort them to the hospital, and have the perimeter secured. Sheldon's concerned that something doesn't seem right. Kate isn't to be left alone or out of anyone's sight. If she has to pee someone's with her," I say.

"I'm all over it, give me a bit and I'll call you back," he says, disconnecting.

"I hate being this far away from Kate when she's going through this all alone. Any possibility we can go to the hospital?" Jenny says.

"Yes, but I want more specifics before we go. We'll plan to leave tomorrow once we know security is in place and it isn't a ruse to get everyone under one roof," he says.

"God, I didn't even think about that," she says, curling in next to me on the sofa.

"Yeah, I'm hoping that Chase connects and we learn more tonight but until then we need to wait it out," I say and she nods.

"In the meantime, I'm pretty sure we can find something to do," I say, scooping her into my arms and carrying her into my bedroom.

TWENTY-FIVE

JENNY

I awaken hours later entwined in his arms, slip out of his embrace and pad into the bathroom. When I return to the bedroom the city around us filters enough light into the room to view him splayed out on the king size bed. The sheets are twisted and barely reach his waist leaving his silently rising and falling chest on display. His dark hair is over his eyes and the view tugs at my heart. I don't know how this man has come to mean so much to me in such a short time but I know that he has pulled me out of the deepest recesses of darkness and come to mean the world to me.

He turns and reaches onto my side of the bed and pats the emptiness beside him in his sleep. I slip under the sheet and his arms immediately go around my waist pulling me into the protection of his strength. I know that it was difficult for him to tell me he cares and that his actions validate his feelings, but I also know that he has lost everyone in the world that he loved and has experienced things that have left him tainted against love and unwilling to get close to anyone. Even admitting that he cares about me is a huge step for him.

I vow silently not to let what has happened to me keep me away from my loved ones in the future. My mom, my sister, nieces and little nephew and even my brother deserve much better than the way I have treated them in the last few months. I stroke his shoulder and love the way the warmth of his breath feels gently caressing my hair in his sleep and the feel of his arms tightening around me. The beating of his heart is calming, as always, and I nuzzle into his strength but the depth of my feelings scare me. In just a very short time he has managed to help me put myself back together and dispel the darkness that has surrounded me ever since the attack, but I also know he has the power to shatter me in the way that no one else could.

TWENTY-SIX

BRIAN

My cell awakens me and I glance at the time as Scottie's name shows up on the display and answer it, shifting into an upright position against the headboard, slowly so as not to wake Jenny. "Sorry to disrupt your beauty sleep lad, but Sheldon was right. The security lead is dirty, we've got transmissions, granted they've been scrambled, but we were able to connect them from him to two locations where we know Alfreita was last. The hit was an inside job. They knew days if not longer ago that Carlos was planning to take Karissa out last night. It was their anniversary and the bastards crashed into them with a semi-truck. Absolutely nothing left of the vehicle."

"Secure him and get as much information as we can until we know more from Chase and Jay. We can't take the chance that he'll hurt any of Chase's family," I say.

"Will do, boss. You know it's all over the bloody news?"

"Yeah, unfortunate. I was hoping we could intervene but we were too late. It's splashed all over the world."

"Okay, get him secure and talking and keep me updated," I say before disconnecting and looking down at Jenny. She's managed to sleep through my conversation and to me she looks like a fucking dark haired angel.

My cell phone rings again and I glance down irritated, but hit the accept button when I see it is Chase.

"Brian, we got all the messages. We're about thirty minutes outside of New York. What happened?" he says.

"Carlos has a dirty fuckin' head of security that's what. Someone put a hit out on Carlos and Karissa Larussio. They're pretty sure Kate's mom will make it, but it's not looking good for Carlos. Sheldon and Don are with Kate. Jenny and I are flying out later in the day."

"Thanks, Brian. Katarina will need her best friend to get through this," Chase says.

"We'll be there soon. I just needed to be sure there wasn't a plan to get us all in the same spot or we would have flown out last night. Sheldon's been keeping me and Scottie updated and Scottie's team is interrogating the head of security as we speak. We hope to know more details shortly, but from what we know now it was a hit, it was preplanned, an inside job and they took them out with a fucking semi. The scene is a mess. I tried to manage the media, but the entire city was lit up with firetrucks, police cars, and ambulances. Every newscaster within a hundred mile radius was swarming the area so it's all over the news. Kate is fine, she finally fell asleep. Sheldon is with her in her mom's room and Don is with her dad."

"Thanks for everything, Brian. I'll fill you in with what I know when we're together. Let me know what Scottie and his team learn," he says.

"Will do. I hope everything goes okay. We'll be there as soon as we can. I have a couple more things that I need to wrap up before we leave and I don't want Jenny to miss her counseling session this morning," I say.

"Completely understand," he says before disconnecting and I slip under the covers and pull Jenny back into my arms. She shifts as though she's going to wake up but then nuzzles into my chest and makes that little purring sound in her sleep.

Dr. Werther arrives just before eleven a.m. and the visit goes long again. It's almost twelve thirty before they finish. They walk out of my study and I thank her for coming to the penthouse for the session and Matt escorts her downstairs to the driver that will take her home.

Jenny seems quiet when she comes to sit by me on the couch a few minutes later. I close my laptop and lay it on the coffee table. "You okay?" I ask, kissing her lightly on the lips.

"I think so. We talked about a lot of things. Mostly about the day he was in my apartment and what I did," she says.

I'm not sure where this is going. "What do you mean?" I

ask, watching her slip out of her shoes and tuck her little feet underneath her.

"I've never told anyone this but my father taught me how to protect myself, I mean really take care of myself. I haven't really kept refreshed which is why I want to go to a self-defense class."

I'm still not following her train of thought. I'm not sure why she feels the need to justify wanting to attend the training and I told her I'd find the best in the business for her. She's ringing her hands every so often and isn't maintaining eye contact with me. She's nervous about something and it puts me on edge worse than the toughest of global negotiations.

"Tell me what's bothering you."

She nods and licks her lips. "Brian, I wasn't trying to get him off of me when he was tying me up."

I don't like the way that sounds one fucking bit and try to push down all the thoughts that are swirling around in my warped heart. I know she needs to get this off of her chest whether I want to hear it or not. "Tell me," I say, pulling her into my lap half afraid that I'm going to lose my shit over what she's about ready to say.

"I wasn't trying to stop him, Brian," she says and the tears begin to fall. I can feel my insides tighten and my jaw constrict.

"I was trying to kill him but it wasn't quite hard enough," she says, pressing against me, her tears immediately soaking through my dress shirt.

I don't know what I thought she was going to say, but it

wasn't this. She's crying like it's a bad thing and I'm fucking elated that she wanted the bastard dead.

"That's a natural response; of course you wanted him gone after what he did. Does that bother you?" I ask, lifting her chin to me.

She shakes her head. "No, but is it bad that I just wanted to snuff the life right out of him, have no remorse and would do it all over again but better?" she asks.

"I can't even believe you're worrying about that piece of garbage. You have every right to have wanted to kill the fucker, but I'm glad you don't have that blood or the guilt that may have come with it on your hands. I do think it's good that you're talking about it though," I say.

"Me, too," she says, sniffling and wiping her tears. "It's not as hard as it was now that I've let her in a little bit."

"So, does she grill you about your sex life, too?" I ask, trying to lighten her spirits. She punches me half-heartedly.

"She did ask me about us but only related to going from one relationship into another one."

"It's been months," I say, recalling the date of the first attack from Scottie's notes.

"I know, she wasn't opposed at all, just thought I might want to explore my feelings. You know, it's just hard to stop once you get started, so of course I told her everything. She was a little shocked that I love to get my pussy paddled and that you spank me until my ass is bright red and that I like it," she says, looking up at me with those deep green eyes.

"You told her that?"

She smiles and her eyes are alight with mischievousness.

"No, but I did tell her I was exploring my sexuality and she believes that's a positive thing and maybe one of the reasons I feel confident in opening up and fighting back. I'm finding myself."

"Well, Ms. Torzial, any way that I can be of assistance," I say, sliding her skirt up and rubbing her against my growing hardness. I feel her heat as she grinds against me and I groan, lifting the bottom of her shirt up over her tight little abs and waist, slipping her shirt over her head and leaving her in a lacy front closure bra. It takes a mere flick of my fingers to expose her pink perky nipples to my gaze.

She's so fucking submissive in the bedroom and I love it. She knows what she wants, but she wants it with me dominating, controlling the situation and that makes my cock throb. I push her panties to the side and slide my finger along her slippery length. "You're so wet for me, Sweetheart," I say, sinking two fingers deep inside of her. She purrs and in one quick shift, my cock is out, I'm wrapped and I pull her down, seating myself to the root, exploring the heat that it so desperately wants. I guide her, pulling her hips up and down atop my throbbing member, not sure when it's started to be okay to have sex like this, but it sure as shit doesn't feel vanilla when she's riding my cock and her little tits are bouncing in front of me.

I pull her down harder, shifting her hips so that I can hit that special little spot that makes her cry out when her hips are tilted.

Her pussy clenches around me and she starts to moan. "Come for me now," I instruct and she explodes around me, shaking on the end of my cock and it takes everything that I have to hold back until I've made her come two more times and only then do I plow into her and allow my own release.

TWENTY-SEVEN

JENNY

I **am completely exhausted**, emotionally and sexually sated and would like nothing more than to curl up and go to sleep, but Brian swats me on the ass. "Let's get cleaned up, you can sleep on the plane. Everything has been cleared. We're heading to the hospital."

I come alive quickly at the thought of being with my best friend and throw a few things into an overnight bag and it takes less than twenty minutes for security to have us on our way.

As Brian's driver pulls up to the private tarmac at O'Hare we are guided to the white Gulfstream jet that proudly displays the bold blue Carrington Steel logo. The interior is plush and upscale, boasting of a marble black and white bar in the corner, a fifty-inch television monitor, a black leather couch with a zebra patterned throw on the back, and matching chaise in the center of the room.

"It's magnificent," I say, enthralled with all the different designs that can be incorporated into the same model of a Gulfstream.

"You should see the bedroom," he says, taking my hand and leading me into the master suite.

"Whoa, it's seriously over the top," I say, looking around at the chrome headboard, slate wall covering, large monitor overhead, and the bar in the corner.

He smirks. "Well, I'd love to show you how over the top it can get in here, but right now you need to rest. You look exhausted and I have a few calls to make. He slips the sweater dress over my head leaving me in dressy boots and my underwear. His eyes light up as he takes me in. "Well, I could be persuaded to have my evil way with you, but you need to sleep, Sweetheart," he says, unfastening my bra and slipping my panties down past my hips and over my boots. I step out of them.

"I couldn't resist seeing you naked with those boots on," he says. My breath hitches. He's kneeling in front of me and I can feel the warmth of his breath while he slides the zipper down my boot, taking his time before moving to the other. He blows his warm breath there, making my entire body tingle with anticipation and I can't help the moan that slips out.

"Change of plans, Sweetheart. Looks like you're going to be introduced to the mile high experience as part of the Carrington tuck down service," he says, before slipping his tongue over my sensitive clit.

* * *

I wake a short time later feeling sexually sated and rested, and slide up against the headboard, pull the sheet around me, and open my laptop. I peruse email not wanting Kate to have the added pressure of worrying about Torzial on top of everything going on with her parents. It doesn't look overly daunting with mostly just items from last evening and today to sift through. I sit cross-legged in bed using my pillow as a makeshift laptop desk, as I glance through the mail. I click on an older item and gasp as the sender's name shows up.

You appeared a little ashen at last evening's festivities. Perhaps a little too much to drink or were you thinking about something in particular? Perhaps the special night we shared? I sincerely hope that is the case and if so that you continue to dream about that every night until I can repay you for all the joy you have brought me and we can be together again. Until then your secret about Torzial is safe with me.

Yours always, Ty

I skim the email taking note of the send date. Well before he attacked me again but just his name on an email sends me into a panic. Torzial secret, what the fuck? My heart begins to pound and my breathing becomes labored. I know I need to breathe or spin out of control and I am trying my best, but the oxygen just won't sync. I gasp, time and time again, trying to inhale deeply but to no avail.

I hear Brian's voice through the thumping of my heart and pounding in my head. "You're having a panic attack. I want you to concentrate on my voice. I'm going to pick you up now, nod if you understand," he says.

I nod and gulp in a breath of air and squeeze his neck, feeling the safety and security of his arms wrapping tightly around me. "Good, now we're going to count backward from ten," he says, rubbing my back as we count. I focus on the sound of his voice and the warmth of his hand making patterns along my shoulder blades and spine and my breathing finally starts to normalize.

"Come back to me Sweetheart," I hear, feeling his warm breath against my hair. All I want is to feel his body closer to mine and I nuzzle into his strength listening to the calming sound of his heartbeat.

"You wanna tell me what's been going on inside of that gorgeous little mind of yours?" he asks, kissing me lightly on the lips. The voice, although seemingly at a distance, pulls me back and the feel of his lips urges me to take a deep breath and feel his warmth against me.

"Sweetheart," he murmurs and I feel myself opening. "That's it baby, let me in. Tell me what's going on," he says.

"I was reading emails and there was one from Ty. It was from before the attack but I didn't see it until now. Just seeing it brought everything flooding back," I say, wiping the tears from my eyes, angry that he has made me this weak again.

"Shh. It's a completely normal response," he says, pulling me close.

I nod still feeling embarrassed that just an email from the bastard can get in my head like that and cause me to lose my ability to even breathe. I put my arms around his neck and pull him tight to me. He is my rock and I don't know what I would do without him. "He said my secret about Torzial was safe with him and then I recalled him saying that he was at my townhouse to put something on my computer to make sure everyone knew I was guilty. It sort of freaked me out but then I remembered that whatever he was doing was interrupted when I walked in."

He nods and pulls me tighter against him. "I was going to tell you when we got home from the hospital later today, but he will never, ever, be able to hurt you again, Sweetheart. I just received word that he was found dead earlier this morning," he says.

"Ty is dead? What happened?" I ask, unable to stem the extreme cold and trembling that overtakes my body as Brian holds me close.

"He apparently messed with the wrong people, Sweetheart. He was found dead with his member in his mouth. It sounds like it may have been a mafia hit, but he will never bother you again. No more emails, no threats, nothing," he says, kissing my lips gently.

"I know I should feel bad, but I don't. He was going to come after me again. He was going to hurt me again," I say, frantically trying to control the tidal wave of tears.

"He's gone, Sweetheart. Nothing to worry about now, it's finally over," he says, caressing my cheek and wiping my tears with his hand.

"Thank you for everything you did to protect me from him. I know I should be sorry that he's gone. He once meant a great deal to me. He gave me a heart-shaped locket and told me that he loved me, but then turned into a monster and broke my heart. All I feel is a great sense of relief," I say.

The intensity of his gaze holds mine. "He got what he had coming and you deserve so much better. Now we should get ready so we can get to the hospital and you can visit with Kate. We'll have our bags taken to my penthouse and stay there tonight," he says, pushing my hair behind my ear.

"How many buildings do you own?" I ask.

"Including yours?" he asks, smirking at me and running his fingers down the side of my neck and under the sheet that he has wrapped around my nakedness.

"Well yes, including that one, smart ass," I say.

"I'm glad to see that you've gotten that sassy little tongue of yours back," he says, flipping me and smacking my ass with the palm of his hand.

"Ouch," I squeal, caught off guard. "You didn't answer my question," I say.

"No, I didn't. Probably more than I should but it makes traveling easier and I can work anywhere with today's technological capabilities," he says.

I nod. "I usually can, too, but I'll probably need to spend a little more time at the New York and L.A locations the next six months. Kate will be able to manage all the Vegas expansion work for Prestian Corp and the Larussios while I focus on expanding Torzial," I say.

"It just so happens one of my nicer condos is in L.A. and my estate happens to be in Bel Air. In fact, I can't wait for you to see it. It was created as a playground for the rich and elite of Hollywood to spend time acting out their fantasies, safe and secure from the paparazzi and limelight. Let's just say it's a bit over the top and I can't wait for you to experience it. We'll travel back and forth as necessary. It won't be a problem."

"I would love to see your home, Brian, but I didn't bring it up looking for you to take care of me. I know it doesn't seem like it after what just happened, but I'm getting stronger. I'll be able to manage on my own," I say.

"I don't think you've been listening if you think for one minute that I'm about to let you go traipsing all over the country without me. When I said you were mine, I meant it. I want you curled up on my chest when I wake up in the morning and my arms wrapped around you when I go to sleep at night."

* * *

Please consider leaving a review if you liked the story. Reviews are like hugs, and I'm hugging you right back for being awesome!

NOTE FROM THE AUTHOR

A sincere thank you for reading and to everyone for all of the words of encouragement received while writing Jenny and Brian's story. I hope you have enjoyed it and are looking forward to learning what happens as their relationship develops, they deal with the fallout of Ty's death, Brian exposes her to his mansion and playground in Bel Air, and so much more.

If you liked the story, a review on Amazon would be greatly appreciated. It is a wonderful way to share your opinions with others who may be looking for a novel to read, but please no spoilers.

If you are interested in following my work, keeping apprised of new contests, title announcements, cover reveals and release dates, please feel free to connect with me on:

Facebook https://www.facebook.com/ViaMariAuthor/

Twitter https://twitter.com/ViaMari_Writer
Instagram https://www.instagram.com/viamari.inc/
Amazon http://amzn.to/2lnGMpJ
Website http://www.viamariauthor.com/

Thanks!

Via

VIA MARI'S BOOKS CHRONOLOGY

The books of all of Via's series:

THE PRESTIAN SERIES

THE TORZIAL AFFAIR

BILLIONAIRE BODYGUARDS, AND

THE LARUSSIO LEGACY

are set in the same universe, with overlapping characters, settings, and events.

Read them in order!

Or jump around, following characters you love!

THE PRESTIAN SERIES

Degrees of Innocence*-Chase & Katarina*

Degrees of Acceptance*-Chase & Katarina*

Degrees of Control*-Chase & Katarina*

Degrees of Power*-Chase & Katarina*

THE TORZIAL AFFAIR SERIES:

Shattered *-Jenny & Brian*

Bound *-Jenny & Brian*

Claimed -*Jenny & Brian*

BILLIONAIRE BODYGUARDS SERIES:

Wayward -*Jay & Sasha*

Undercover -*Matt & Marenah*

Auctioned -*Damian & Brianna-coming soon*

Relentless -*Dereck & Layla-coming soon*

THE LARUSSIO LEGACY SERIES:

Rule -*Chase & Katarina,*

and Gio & Serena

Rise - *Gio & Serena*

Reign -*Gio & Serena,*

plus Jay

ACKNOWLEDGMENTS

I will always be grateful to the following people for their dedication and the support they have provided along the way:

Wayne, my husband, thank you for always believing in me, supporting my passions, and helping me make my crazy dream come true.

My parents and family who have been a solid and steady reminder that goals can be achieved with determination, hard work, and commitment.

Karla, my dear friend, thank you, for your unconditional support! Who read the first book first and encouraged me to keep going. Who also recommended getting other beta readers, because, "You can only read a book for the first time, once."

Debbie, my dear friend, thank you, for your encouragement and willingness to tour Chicago and New York with me while researching for the story!

Debbie, my dearest editor, thank you, for putting hours and hours into these books, carefully poring over them to ensure the reader has a wonderful experience.

Tonia, Roslynn, Carryl and Deb, our mastermind group, thank you, for the endless hours of dedication to each of our goals. I would not be here without you!

The readers, beta readers, bloggers, and social media friends whose support has made the hard work worthwhile.

ABOUT THE AUTHOR

Contemporary romantic suspense author Via Mari likes to keep her readers on the edge, fanning themselves as the action unfolds and the heat rises. Her books, featuring the most handsome alpha billionaires, elite bodyguards, and powerful mafiosi, exemplify extreme romance, with dominant men who stop at nothing to protect the women they love.

Via likes to push boundaries (as do her alphas!), delving into relationships with power exchanges, exploring the differences, similarities and extreme levels of trust required of the individuals, and reveling in the deep desires that drive Dominant/submissive relationships.

Via was raised in both the United States and United Kingdom, and she enjoys exploring new places. Since childhood, she has enjoyed reading books that carry you away. In fact, you can still find her in the early hours of the morning, curled up in an overstuffed chair by a crackling wood fire, reading a page-turning novel, especially during the harsh winters of the Midwestern United States.

When not writing, Via spends her days with her husband and

family, including an adorable fur-baby. She enjoys gardening, shopping at the local farmers market, and walking for exercise in town or around a big city. And she loves traveling to research her next novel.

Most of all, Via loves to spend time interacting with you, her readers, so feel free to connect with her on the following social media sites!

Facebook @ViaMariAuthor
Twitter @ViaMari_Writer

Made in the USA
Middletown, DE
13 June 2023

32544311R00166